For more than forty years,
Yearling has been the leading name
in classic and award-winning literature
for young readers.

Yearling books feature children's
favorite authors and characters,
providing dynamic stories of adventure,
humor, history, mystery, and fantasy.

Trust Yearling paperbacks to entertain,
inspire, and promote the love of reading
in all children.

OTHER YEARLING BOOKS YOU WILL ENJOY

HOOT, *Carl Hiaasen*

SWEAR TO HOWDY, *Wendelin Van Draanen*

HOLES, *Louis Sachar*

BUD, NOT BUDDY, *Christopher Paul Curtis*

THE TRIAL, *Jen Bryant*

THE CRICKET IN TIMES SQUARE, *George Selden*

THE PHANTOM TOLLBOOTH, *Norton Juster*

VOYAGE OF ICE, *Michele Torrey*

THE DARK-THIRTY: SOUTHERN TALES OF
THE SUPERNATURAL, *Patricia C. McKissack*

THE LEGACY OF GLORIA RUSSELL, *Sheri Gilbert*

JOHN FEINSTEIN

LAST SHOT

A FINAL FOUR MYSTERY

A YEARLING BOOK

Published by Yearling, an imprint of Random House Children's Books
a division of Random House, Inc., New York

Visit us on the Web! www.randomhouse.com/kids

Educators and librarians, for a variety of teaching tools, visit us at
www.randomhouse.com/teachers

ISBN-13: 978-0-553-49460-0
ISBN-10: 0-553-49460-0

Reprinted by arrangement with Alfred A. Knopf Books for Young Readers

Printed in the United States of America

August 2006

10 9

This is for Danny and Brigid,
my favorite young readers and future journalists

ACKNOWLEDGMENTS

Every book is a collaborative effort, none more so than this one. Esther Newberg, my tireless and remarkably stubborn agent, was the first person to suggest the notion of a children's book to me and her assistants, Andrea Barzvi and Christine Bauch, pushed me forward until I jumped off the cliff and made the attempt.

I was more than fortunate that Nancy Siscoe at Knopf saw potential in the idea and then pushed, prodded, and pulled until there was actually a book. A good editor needs a great deal of patience; Nancy has plenty of that, but also a creative mind that, even as I benefitted from it, made me quite envious.

My friends and family occasionally roll their eyes when I try new things but are always there to support me when I attempt them. That was especially true in this case of Mary, my wife, and Danny and Brigid, who each have a good deal in common with this book's two young heroes. . . .

Steven Thomas
735 Northview Blvd.
Norristown, PA 19401

Dear Steven Thomas:

It is my great pleasure to inform you that you have been selected
by the U.S. Basketball Writers Association as one of the two
winners in this year's USBWA fourteen-and-under writing
contest. Your story "Nothing Like the Palestra" was selected by
the judges from more than 200 entries. Congratulations! You
and your co-winner, Susan Carol Anderson, will be flown,
courtesy of the USBWA, to New Orleans to participate as
working journalists at this year's Final Four. Press credentials
and a hotel room have been arranged for you and a guardian,
and our executive director, Joe Mitch, will be in touch with you
shortly to arrange flights and to answer any questions about
your schedule, attached here. You should plan on arriving no
later than Thursday evening, since the presentation of your
award will take place Friday morning. We hope you stay right
through the championship game on Monday night. We look
forward to seeing you in New Orleans at what we all hope will
be just the first of many Final Fours you will cover in your
journalism career.

Again, congratulations on a wonderfully reported and
written story.

Best wishes,

Bobby Kelleher
President, USBWA

1: THE LETTER

STEVIE THOMAS read the letter once, then twice, then a third time to be sure it was real. Then he started screaming.

"Mom! Mom! Mom!"

Stevie suffered a few bad moments when his mom said she wasn't sure she or his father could get away from work to go with him and then started fussing about the time off from school. But somehow Stevie knew his dad wasn't going to turn this down.

After all, Bill Thomas had been the one who had first introduced his son to sports—specifically basketball. He had started taking Stevie to see Philadelphia's Big Five—Temple, Villanova, St. Joseph's, Pennsylvania, and La Salle—when he was four. Going to basketball games had become Bill and Stevie's thing. Occasionally they went to see the 76ers play but neither of them thought the NBA was really worth their time. Stevie had written a story for his school's monthly newspaper, the *Main Line Chronicle*, about watching players on the 76ers bench sit and laugh and tell jokes during the last few minutes of a 20-point loss to the woeful Washington Wizards. But the college players really cared.

It was through the *Chronicle* that he had heard about the USBWA writing contest. The paper had received a press release inviting anyone age fourteen and under to enter the contest. What got Stevie's attention was the line at the bottom of the release: "Two winners will be chosen to fly to New Orleans to be members of the working press during the Final Four." Right there in one sentence were both his dreams come true: a chance to go to the Final Four *and* to go there with a press pass.

Stevie had taught himself to read at age five using the sports section, so the reporters were as big heroes to him as the players and coaches. His favorite Philly reporter was Dick Jerardi. But it wasn't long before he learned he could call up stories from other papers online and read Mike Lupica and Dick Weiss from the New York *Daily News* and his two heroes, Tony Kornheiser and Mike Wilbon, who he knew worked for the *Washington Post*, since he watched them every day on *Pardon the Interruption*.

Stevie wanted to really impress the judges with his reporting skills, so he called the main number at the *Daily News* and asked to speak to Dick Jerardi. To his delight, Jerardi called him back the next day, and when he explained that he wanted to write a story about the Palestra,

Jerardi gave him the names and phone numbers for all the local SIDs—short for Sports Information Directors—who could help him with his story.

Shaun May, the SID (Stevie liked using the term; it made him feel like a pro) at Penn, gave him a press credential to cover the Penn-Columbia game. Stevie and his dad had gone to the Palestra a million times before, but this time his dad was in the bleachers—and Stevie was on press row. He decided that night, even before sitting down to write the story, that this was definitely what he wanted to do when he grew up. Get paid to have the best seats at a basketball game? Get to talk to the players and interview Coach Fran Dunphy? Have someone bring statistics to your seat at every time-out? Eat for free in the pressroom before the game?

"Dad, why would anyone want to do anything else?"

His father, who worked in a large law firm downtown, nodded. "I've thought about that more than once myself," he said. "Of course, you know, sportswriters don't make very much money."

"Kornheiser and Wilbon do," Stevie answered. "Lupica does."

"That's three out of thousands," his dad answered. "And they only make big money because they're on TV."

He had a point. But still, if you could get paid at all to go to games and have the best seats, you were pretty lucky.

Stevie spent hours putting together his story, making the Palestra the feature, rather than the game. He poured ten years' worth of avid fandom into his writing, and when he was finished he had almost three thousand words. The contest rules said no more than one thousand. Cutting two-thirds of what he had written was painful, but he thought the end result was pretty strong. He sent the story in just before the January 15 deadline and waited, hoping against hope he might win.

Now he had to wait until his father came home to make it official. Naturally, he was late. It was almost seven by the time he heard the car pull into the garage. Stevie was waiting for him, letter in hand, when his dad walked inside.

"Nice to see you, too," he said as Stevie thrust the letter at him without saying hello. But then he started to read.

"*Wow!*" he said. "Stevie, that's really great! I'm so proud of you!"

"So I can go?" Stevie said.

"What did your mother say?"

"She said I can go if you can go with me."

Dad smiled. "I think that could be arranged. I'm sure I could scalp a ticket down there if I had to."

"Scalp what?" Mom said, walking into the room.

"A ticket to get into the Final Four," Dad said, waving the letter.

"What about work for you and school for Stevie?"

"Hon, this is a once-in-a-lifetime chance. Plus, he earned it by winning the contest. I really think he'll learn a lot from the trip."

She smiled. "Uh-huh. And clearly you won't mind going either."

"Not even a little bit."

And so it was settled. But Stevie knew his dad was

wrong about one thing. This would *not* be a once-in-a-lifetime experience. For him, it would be a *first*-in-a-lifetime experience.

He would see to that.

■ ■ ■

If Stevie had been in charge, he and his dad would have flown to New Orleans on the first flight available on Thursday morning. That would have given them all afternoon to hang out at the coaches' hotel.

"The coaches' hotel? What in the world is that?" his father asked when Stevie broached the idea.

"*All* the basketball coaches in the world go to the Final Four," Stevie said. "It's like a convention or something. And there's this one hotel where they all stay and hang out. I mean, except for the four whose teams are playing."

"How do you know all this?"

"I read it in that book you gave me for Christmas last year."

"I should have known."

But it turned out six-thirty was the earliest his dad could get away. They connected in Atlanta and arrived at the hotel a few minutes after eleven, which with the time change meant it was after midnight on Stevie's body clock. Still, when he and his dad walked into the sparkling lobby of the New Orleans Hyatt Regency, he forgot how tired he was. A large sign just inside the door said WELCOME FINAL FOUR MEDIA. Proud and still a little amazed, Stevie thought to himself: That's me.

They made their way to the front desk to check in. There was only one person working and the man ahead of them was engaged in a loud argument with that person.

"Look, I've been in the car for fourteen hours today," Stevie heard the man say. "I really don't need this. I *know* my reservation was for a suite. I don't want one of those tiny little rooms you give to people. I didn't come here to spend five days sleeping in a closet."

"Sir, this is a king-size room. And, as I said, if we can upgrade you tomorrow, we will. You can speak to the manager about the confusion in your reservation in the morning."

"Confusion?" the man shouted. "There's no confusion. You screwed up. This is outrageous. I mean, don't you have any idea who I am?"

Suddenly, Stevie knew exactly who the man was.

"Dad," he hissed, "that's Tony Kornheiser!"

His dad smiled. "Sounds like he's having a bad night."

At that moment, Kornheiser turned around and looked at them. "I'm really sorry about this. They screwed up my reservation."

Disgusted, he took the key that the clerk was now handing him. "This isn't the end of this," he said to the clerk. "Have a good night," he said to Stevie and his dad as he walked toward the elevators.

"You too, Mr. Kornheiser," Stevie said. "I hope the rest of the weekend gets better for you."

Kornheiser stopped and smiled at Stevie. He pointed at the clerk, then at Stevie. "You see," he said, "*he* knows who I am."

He turned and walked away.

"Dad," Stevie said with a grin, "I have a feeling this is going to be the most unbelievable weekend of my life."

2: THE OTHER WINNER

STEVIE WAS UP AT SEVEN the next morning, barely able to control his excitement. The first event on their agenda was the USBWA awards breakfast, where he and his co-winner, Susan Carol Anderson, would receive their plaques and meet their escorts for the weekend. According to the USBWA press release that had been waiting for them in their room, Susan Carol was from Goldsboro, North Carolina.

"I just hope," he said to his father, "that she's not a Duke fan."

"If she's from North Carolina, she probably likes Duke or North Carolina," his dad said.

Whatever. Susan Carol wasn't who he wanted to meet anyway. The USBWA would also be giving out its Player of the Year and Coach of the Year awards. Paul Hewitt, the coach at Georgia Tech, whose team had lost to Connecticut in the East Regional final, had won the coaching award, and Raymond Felton, the great guard from North Carolina, was the Player of the Year. Since the Tar Heels had been upset by Saint Joseph's in round sixteen, Felton would also be there.

This was almost a perfect Final Four as far as Stevie was concerned. There was a Philadelphia team—St. Joe's—which made him happy. There was a Big East team—Connecticut—which also made him happy, since the Big East was his favorite league. There was a Big Ten team—Minnesota State—which was okay with him, especially since he absolutely loved to watch Chip Graber play. If Stevie could wake up one morning and be anybody in the world, it would be Chip Graber. Graber was only five eleven, but he was, as Dick Vitale always said on TV, "an absolute jet." A little guy who went past people before they knew what had happened. Chip was a senior, and his dad, Alan Graber, was his coach. That father-son story line made MSU the media's favorite team. Stevie had read that Graber might be one of the first five players chosen in the NBA draft in spite of his height. Some people called him "Iverson without the tattoos." He was that good.

Stevie had grown three inches in eighth grade, so he was now five foot four. Short, and not even close to being a jet. More like a prop plane. He had made the eighth-grade team at school, but he only got to play when the team was way ahead or way behind.

"My ability in this sport," he had announced to his dad after a game in which he never moved off the bench, "is limited to knowing the difference between a good player and a bad player."

"Which puts you ahead of quite a few people," his father pointed out.

The only team that had made it to New Orleans that bothered Stevie was Duke. The dreaded Blue Devils, who *always* seemed to be in the Final Four. Or close to it. Every time he turned on ESPN, it seemed as if Dick Vitale or someone else was yelling about how great Duke was and how Mike Krzyzewski was the most wonderful coach and the best person who had ever lived.

Yech.

Okay, he was a pretty good coach—ten Final Fours, three national titles. But there was something really annoying about a team that never lost. And Duke always got the calls from the referees, especially when they played Maryland, and Maryland was Stevie's favorite ACC team. Stevie had hoped against hope that Villanova would beat Duke in the Sweet Sixteen, but it hadn't happened. Then Duke had come from 13 points down in the regional final to beat Louisville. Now Duke was slated to play Connecticut in the second game on Saturday, after Minnesota State and St. Joe's faced off in the first game. The winners of those games would play for the national championship on Monday night.

Getting off the elevator for breakfast, Stevie spotted someone wearing a button that said "ABD" on it. "Hey," he said, "what team is that?"

The woman wearing the button smiled at him and said, "It means 'Anybody But Duke.'"

"I want one of those," Stevie said to his dad as they walked toward the ballroom.

"Might blow your unbiased-reporter image, don't you think?"

"I'll wear it inside my shirt, next to my heart."

His dad laughed.

They were met at the ballroom door by a man with a mustache and glasses. "Steven? Mr. Thomas?" he asked as they walked up. "I'm Joe Mitch. We're so glad you could make it."

They shook hands, and Joe Mitch guided them into the room. "Steven, I was one of the judges on the contest. I can't tell you how impressed we all were with your story. Let's go up front. I want you to meet Susan Carol and her dad. They just got here."

Stevie really wanted to meet Paul Hewitt and Raymond Felton and some of the real writers. "We met Tony Kornheiser last night," he said to Mitch. "Sort of."

"Well, you'll meet a lot more people today, I promise you that," Mitch said. "Here are the Andersons."

Stevie braked to a halt when Susan Carol Anderson, hearing her last name, turned around.

The first thing he noticed was that she was about nine feet tall. He looked down at her feet, figuring she was wearing heels. More bad news. She was wearing flats.

"Steven and Bill Thomas," Mitch said. "Susan Carol and Don Anderson."

There were handshakes all around, and Stevie's dad asked Don Anderson how their trip to New Orleans had been. "Not bad," he said. "And you?"

Susan Carol was eyeing him. Stevie stood up as straight as he could. He figured she was about three inches taller than he was. Okay, maybe four. She had long brown hair and, he had to admit, she was pretty . . . for a giraffe. "I read your story," she said. "The one that won. It was very good. I'd like to go to the Palestra someday."

She had one of those Southern accents that stretched words out. "Palestra," in her accent, became *Paa-lae-sta-ra.* Four syllables. At least.

"Thanks," he said. "When did you get a chance to see it?"

"Oh, it's up front," she said. "They blew both our stories up and put them on easels near the podium. Come on, I'll show you."

He had to admit he wanted to see that. "Dad, I'll be up front," he said. His father, Joe Mitch, and Don Anderson were chatting away. His father waved and nodded, and Stevie followed Susan Carol to the front of the room, weaving through people. The stories, as she had reported, were sitting on easels, printed like real newspaper stories. "Wow," he said. "I wish I could get one of those."

"You will," she said. "Mr. Mitch told me they were for us to take home after the breakfast."

"Wow," he said, then realized he had said "wow" twice and probably sounded like a little kid. "I mean, that's really nice of them."

He had been looking at his story, which had been given the headline THE PALESTRA—STILL ROCKING AFTER 80 YEARS, wanting to drink it all in. He looked over at the other easel, where her story was set up. The headline almost made him gag: COACH K—HALL OF FAME COACH . . . AND PERSON.

"So, I guess you're a Duke fan," he said, not bothering to look at what she had actually written.

Her face lit up. "Oh, absolutely." (It came out *abb-so-looo-taly*.) "My daddy went to divinity school there and I've (*aaahv*) been a fan, I guess, since the cradle. I even got to talk to Coach K for my (*mah*) story. He was sooooo nice."

Stevie felt sooooo nauseous. To steer the conversation away from the saintly Coach K, he said, "Your father went to divinity school?"

"Yes," she said. "He's a minister."

"But he's not . . ."

"Dressed like a minister? No. It's mostly priests who wear collars. He wears civilian clothes all the time."

A minister's daughter and a Blue Devils fan . . . Stevie had a thought that made him smile.

"I hear Coach K curses all the time. What does your dad think about that?"

"That even Coach K isn't perfect," she answered, not seeming even a little bit riled by his gibe at the saint.

Someone came up behind them.

"So, I presume you are our two winners. I've read the stories. They're vurry, vurry good."

Stevie knew a Philadelphia accent when he heard it. He

turned and there was Dick "Hoops" Weiss, who had been a legend at the *Philadelphia Daily News* for years before moving to the New York *Daily News*.

"Dick Weiss," he said, introducing himself to Stevie and Susan Carol. "Steven, as a Philly guy, I loved your story on the Palestra, okay? But Susan Carol, you did a great job with Coach K, too." They both thanked him. Weiss explained that they would be given their awards by Bobby Kelleher, the *Washington Herald* columnist who was the president of the USBWA. "After breakfast we'll meet in the lobby at eleven-thirty and head over to the Superdome," he said. "Steven, I'm your escort. Susan Carol, you're going to be with Bill Brill, who is a member of our Hall of Fame. . . ."

"Oh, I know *just* who Bill Brill is," Susan Carol said. "I started reading his stories when I was little. He's fantastic."

Weiss laughed. "Well, one thing I can tell you for sure. He shares your affection for Coach K. And for Duke."

Stevie was about to say something when Bill Brill walked up—he knew it was Bill Brill because he was wearing a name tag on his checked sports coat, which had the widest lapels Stevie had ever seen.

"Hoops, are these our guys?" Brill said.

"Yup. These are the winners."

"Well, congratulations to you both. Susan Carol, you're with me today," Brill said. "I hope you'll be ready to go by eleven."

"Eleven?" Weiss said. "The first practice isn't until noon and it's a five-minute walk to the Dome."

"True," Brill said. "But we have to pick up our credentials

and the kids' credentials. *And* we have to deal with all the new security checks."

"*And* Duke is practicing first," Weiss said, laughing.

"Uh, true," Brill said, reddening slightly.

"Don't feel bad, Mr. Brill," Susan Carol said. "All right-thinking people are Duke fans."

"I can see you two will get along just fine," Weiss said. "Come on, Steven. I'll introduce you to Paul Hewitt. We'll see you guys over at the Dome."

Stevie breathed a sigh of relief as he and Weiss walked away from Brill and Susan Carol.

"God, I thought I was going to throw up with all that Duke stuff," he said to Weiss, feeling he had found a comrade in anti-Duke arms.

"Did you read Susan Carol's story?" Weiss asked.

Stevie grinned. "No," he said. "Was it gross? Nothing but a Coach K love-in?"

"Actually," Weiss said, "it was vurry, vurry good. Might even convert a skeptic like you. She's a talented writer."

Stevie groaned. Nine feet tall *and* a talented writer. Great. Just great.

3: DICK VITALE, BABEEE!

ONCE EVERYONE WAS SEATED, the breakfast didn't take very long. Stevie calculated that the two acceptance speeches lasted about ninety seconds—seventy-five of them for Paul Hewitt; no more than fifteen for Raymond Felton, who thanked his teammates and his coach and sat down. Bobby Kelleher introduced both Stevie and Susan Carol, complimented them on the quality of their work, and then talked about how important the writing contest was because it was vital that older writers encourage younger writers.

"We've got too many kids today who want to grow up and be on television," he said. "There's nothing wrong with TV work except that it's shallow and requires that you spend most of your life screaming into a microphone about how great every coach is. We need to encourage real reporting because it's important."

Stevie was relieved when neither he nor Susan Carol was asked to speak. They just had to pose with their plaques and Kelleher for a couple of pictures. It was almost eleven o'clock by the time the breakfast was over. Weiss found him as he and his dad were heading for the door. Stevie introduced him to his father. "Read you as a kid," Bill Thomas said, shaking Weiss's hand.

"You're making me feel old, okay?" Weiss said, laughing.

He then suggested to Stevie that they meet in the lobby in about fifteen minutes. "Did you bring a laptop?" he asked.

Stevie said he had. The USBWA had made arrangements with twenty small-town papers that couldn't afford to cover the Final Four to use Stevie and Susan Carol as their correspondents for the weekend. They were supposed to write features—one story each day, beginning today.

"Once you decide what you want to write about today, I think it will be easier to do it from the Dome than from back in your room," Weiss said. "Have you ever written on deadline before?"

"Only when he waits until the last minute to finish a paper for school," his father answered.

"I remember that feeling," Weiss said. "You'll be fine. I'll be there to help and there will be guys all over who can feed you quotes if you need them."

Stevie had already given some thought to what he would write. His first idea was a story describing his impressions— what it was like to be at the Final Four with a press pass for the first time. But then he decided that would make him sound like a wide-eyed little kid. He had thought about profiling a benchwarmer, or maybe about how each practice that afternoon was different. Or maybe he would try to talk to some fans about what it meant to *them* to be at a Final Four. They were all decent ideas, but his secret wish was to do a feature on Chip Graber—you had to root for the short guy.

"One thing you ought to do," Weiss added, "is talk to Susan Carol to make sure you don't write the same type of story."

Stevie nodded. He told Weiss he would go get his computer, then he and his dad headed to the elevator. The Andersons were standing there waiting. "I guess we need to bring our computers to the Dome," Stevie said. "Mr. Weiss said it would be easier to write our stories from there."

"Oh, well, I guess you should," Susan Carol said. "But I've already written my story for today."

"You have?"

"Yes, well, the people at Duke were so nice to me when I did my story on Coach K, so I called on Monday and asked if there was *any* way at all to get an interview with Coach Boeheim from Syracuse to find out how he feels being here after finally winning the championship a couple of years ago. Well, Coach K is a friend of his, and he actually called him for me, and I met with Coach Boeheim yesterday afternoon at his hotel! He could *not* have been nicer. So, I wrote my story last night."

"Knowing Coach K was certainly a big help," said Mr. Anderson.

"I guess the key to success is knowing Coach K," Stevie said.

His father gave him a sharp look. The Andersons said nothing. Fortunately, they had reached their floor and were able to escape into the hallway.

"That was a snotty thing to say," Bill Thomas said.

"Yeah, I know. But Dad, how much of that Coach K stuff can you take?"

"Well, it *was* nice of him to help her out. And give her credit. She got an interview with Jim Boeheim because of him. It was a good idea."

Stevie groaned. This fair-and-unbiased-reporter thing was harder than it looked.

■ ■ ■

Things got better once he and Hoops began their walk over to the Dome. It was a perfect early-spring day and the ramp leading from the hotel to the Superdome was filled with people: fans in the colors of the four teams were everywhere; vendors hawked "official" Final Four memorabilia; and every few yards they would walk past someone with a cell phone in one hand and tickets in the other. "Anybody selling?" they would ask.

"Why are they trying to buy tickets?" Stevie asked Weiss, who laughed at the question.

"They're not trying to buy tickets," Weiss answered. "They're scalpers."

"Then why are they asking if people are selling?"

"It's a code they use in case there's an undercover cop around. It's illegal to solicit someone to buy a scalped ticket in Louisiana. But not to ask if someone wants to sell *them* a ticket."

"But you can see they've got tickets in their hands."

"Right. So if someone is looking to buy, they just stop and say, 'I'm buying.' Then they go off someplace quiet and make the sale."

"How much are people paying for the tickets?"

"Someone told me yesterday the scalpers were getting twenty-five hundred bucks a ticket downstairs; closer to fifteen hundred upstairs."

Stevie's mouth dropped open. "Oh my God! My dad was going to try to get a ticket—what's the lowest price? How much do they normally cost?"

"I think it's two hundred and fifty bucks for downstairs. Of course, most people who get the chance to buy tickets paid a lot more for the *right* to buy those tickets in the first place."

"Huh?" People paying for the right to pay for something?

"Most people who get tickets go through the schools that make the Final Four," Weiss explained. "Even though there are sixty-five thousand seats in the Dome, most of them are so far away from the court, you can barely see. The really good seats go to the coaches' association, the NCAA for its sponsors, and to the schools. The way the schools decide who gets to buy the tickets they are allotted is by how much people contribute to their athletic department."

"How much do you have to contribute to buy tickets?"

Weiss shrugged. "Usually at least fifty thousand dollars."

"Each?"

"Yup."

Stevie shook his head in wonderment. "Must be some rich people."

"At the Final Four," Weiss said, "there are no poor people."

"What about students?" Stevie asked. "*They* can't pay fifty thousand dollars."

"No, they can't," Weiss said. "Which is why each school usually only sells about seventy-five to a hundred student tickets."

They had reached the ramp leading up to the walkway that, according to the signs, would take them to the media entrance. Another cell-phone-carrying man approached. "You guys selling?" he asked. He was wearing a white cowboy hat, black leather pants, and cowboy boots.

Weiss smiled and stopped. "If we were selling, how much would you be paying?" he said.

The man eyed Weiss suspiciously from under the cowboy hat. "You a cop?" he asked.

"No, not a cop, a reporter," Weiss said. "I'd just like to know how much you guys are getting."

The scalper smiled and looked behind him for a minute. "What we're asking may be different than what we're getting," he said. "I got seats in the lower bowl, twenty rows up from midcourt, that I'm hoping to get three grand apiece for."

Stevie almost gagged. Three thousand dollars? For one ticket?

"People paying it?" Weiss asked.

"Not right now," the scalper said. "But it's early. By Saturday morning, I'll get it. Maybe more. If you know anybody, tell 'em to look for Big Tex. They'll know me by the hat."

"Big Tex" was about Stevie's height. He wondered how Susan Carol Anderson would react to meeting Big Tex and vice versa.

"I'll be sure to tell them to look for you," Weiss said.

"You do that," Big Tex said. He reached into his pocket, produced a card, and handed it to Weiss, who looked at it, smiled, and passed it on to Stevie. There was a big white cowboy hat on it with the words "Big Tex" in red letters. At the bottom was a phone number. "That's this," Big Tex said, as if reading Stevie's mind, holding the cell phone up. "I got it on all the time."

Stevie stuck the card into his back pocket and they moved on.

"If you want to do a piece that's a little different, you might talk to some of these scalpers," Weiss said. "I guarantee you they've got some stories to tell, okay?"

Yeah right, Stevie thought. Susan Carol would be sending an exclusive Jim Boeheim interview, and he would respond with a Big Tex interview. That would really impress people.

"I'll give it some thought," he said.

Weiss laughed. "No you won't. You're going to want to write about the people inside this place, not the ones outside."

Stevie breathed a sigh of relief. He had thought for a

second Weiss was going to push him to chase down Big Tex. They made it to the door labeled MEDIA ENTRANCE without any further encounters with scalpers or anyone else dressed in loud colors or cowboy hats. They had to wait in line for a few minutes because the security people were checking everyone's bags and wanding people the way they did in airports. Weiss sighed as they waited.

"Not like the old days," he said.

"What was it like in the old days?" Stevie asked.

Weiss laughed. "Where to begin? I'm old enough that I remember when games were played in about ninety minutes," he said.

"Ninety minutes?" Stevie repeated. "How could they possibly have done that?"

"Easy," Weiss said. "There weren't five TV time-outs in every half, and when there was a time-out, it lasted one minute, not three. And halftime didn't take twenty minutes."

Stevie couldn't imagine a college basketball game only taking an hour and a half. To him, anything under two hours and fifteen minutes was a fast game.

The security check didn't take long. Getting their credentials did, because the guy handing them out kept saying he had to see Stevie's driver's license. "It's right in the handbook," he said, producing a phone-book-thick booklet. "You see, it says right here in section eighteen, paragraph three, line four: 'To receive a credential, one must produce a government-issued ID, i.e., driver's license or passport.'"

Weiss rolled his eyes. "Come on, Mike. He's thirteen

years old. He doesn't have a driver's license and probably doesn't have a passport, right?" Stevie nodded to confirm that Weiss was correct. "He's one of the winners of our writing contest. You have a pass there for him. And I'll vouch for him."

The NCAA guy, who was wearing a blue blazer complete with a name tag and a pass dangling around his neck that said "All Access," eyed Stevie and Weiss suspiciously, shaking his head as if to say, *No can do.* "Just because I have a pass for Steven Thomas doesn't mean *he's* Steven Thomas."

"I have my school ID card," Stevie said. "It has a photo on it. They accepted it at the airport."

"Not government-issued," the blue blazer said.

"Hang on a minute," Weiss said. "Stevie, give me your ID."

Stevie pulled out his wallet and handed Weiss the ID. Weiss looked at, turned it over, and smiled. "Look here at the bottom. It says, 'Issued by Montgomery County, Pennsylvania.' He goes to public school. The IDs are issued by the county. That's a government. Hand over his pass."

The blazer took the ID, looked at it for a minute as if it contained hieroglyphics that would unlock the secret to eternal life, then handed it back to Stevie with a disgusted look on his face.

"Okay," he said, riffling through the envelopes and coming up with the one that said "Steven Thomas, USBWA."

"Technically, it is supposed to be a U.S. government ID, but I'll let it slide this once."

"It's that kind of out-of-the-box thinking that makes the NCAA the great organization it is," Weiss said, his voice dripping with sarcasm. Stevie was liking him more every minute. The blazer said nothing. He shoved a pen at Stevie and told him to sign the envelope.

"Next time," he said, "bring your driver's license."

Stevie couldn't resist. "If you can convince my father and the DMV to let me get one when I'm fourteen, I'll gladly bring it," he said.

Before the blazer could reply, Weiss pulled him away and, putting the credentials around their necks, they headed into the building. They followed various signs that pointed them to FLOOR, MEDIA AREAS, and LOCKER ROOMS. They stopped briefly in the huge media work area to drop off their computers, then walked out to the floor. After walking through an empty section of seats that was curtained off from the floor, they maneuvered around the curtain and found themselves at one end of the court.

Stevie had never been inside a dome before. Normally, domes were used for football and seated about 80,000 people. He couldn't get over how big the place was. The entire Palestra would fit into the curtained-off area that wasn't being used. He looked up at the upper-deck seats on the far side of the building. "People sit there?" he said, pointing.

"Absolutely," Weiss said. "And they're thrilled to be there."

"How do they see? It looks like they're about nine miles up."

"They don't," Weiss said. He pointed at the hanging

telescreens that hovered over each end of the court. "They watch the telescreens. I've gone up there. You should take a look at some point. It's even higher than you think."

They walked toward press row, which was filled with people lingering, chatting, killing time. The scoreboard clock read 8:30—and counting down—when Stevie and Hoops walked in. A few Duke players were on the floor, stretching or just talking. Managers stood near a couple of ball racks, as if waiting for their orders.

"What's with the clock?" Stevie asked.

Weiss explained. "They can't start practicing until noon," he said. "Each team gets exactly fifty minutes on the floor. No more, no less. They can't actually touch a basketball until that clock hits zero. And if a coach decides he doesn't want to use the entire fifty minutes, his team has to stay on the floor until the fifty minutes is up, because that's what the rule book says."

"Do they need a government-issued ID to leave?" Stevie asked.

Weiss laughed. Behind them, someone was screaming at him. "Hoops! Hey, Hoops!"

Weiss and Stevie turned in the direction of the voice, and Stevie did a double take when he saw the source of the screaming. It was Dick Vitale, the ESPN announcer and probably the most famous person in the world of college basketball—more famous than Coach K or Bobby Knight and certainly more famous than any of the players. Stevie remembered Dick Jerardi telling him that the most amazing thing about Vitale was that he screamed and bounced off walls as much off the air as he did on the air. "It's not an act," Jerardi had said. "That's who he really is."

"Come on," Weiss said. "I'll introduce you to Dickie V."

"Does he bite?" Stevie asked.

"Nah," Weiss said, "the only thing he might do is break one of your eardrums."

They walked over to a makeshift podium set up on one corner of the court. There was a neon sign on the front of it that said ESPN'S FINAL FOUR FRIDAY. Stevie had completely forgotten that the Final Four was now so big that ESPN actually televised all four *practices* live. As much as he loved basketball, he couldn't imagine sitting around all afternoon watching teams practice and listening to coaches tell Dickie V and his fellow announcers how happy they were to be here.

As Weiss and Stevie approached, Vitale, who had been standing next to the podium, threw his arms open and screamed Weiss's nickname again: "Hoops, my main man, how awesome is it to be in the Big Easy, baby?!!"

He hugged Weiss, who said something Stevie couldn't hear in reply. Then Weiss said, "Dick, I want you to meet one of the winners of our writing contest—this is Steven Thomas. He's a Philly guy."

"Steve, baby!" Vitale screamed, pumping Stevie's hand. "AWESOME to meet you, really AWESOME! Philly, huh? Gotta love the Big Five, baby, right? Who's your favorite team? Saint Joe's, like my Italian paisan Phil Martelli? He's a PTPer, baby, he's one of the best. Lemme tell you another thing, THIS is a PTPer right here, baby, my man Hoops.

You want to be a big-time writer someday? This is the man right here. You just watch him in action, baby. Knows everyone. EVERYONE. Hey, he's written three books on Dickie V! How awesome is that? So who do you like here, Stevie? You gotta love the Dookies, right? Wait, you're from Philly, you're probably a Big East guy! The Huskies, baby, all the way, right?!!"

Stevie was nodding his head, trying to remember what a PTPer was—it came to him, Prime-Time Player—and take in all that Vitale was saying while Vitale was still pumping his hand as if expecting water to come out of it.

Without waiting for Stevie to answer any of his questions, Vitale turned back to Weiss. "Hey, Hoops, did you hear the big rumor? Knight's retiring. Got it from a great source. Check it out."

"You going with it when you go on the air?" Weiss asked.

"No, the source isn't THAT good. Hey, speaking of 'on the air,' we're on in two minutes! Gotta go, baby! Stevie, great talking to you, kid! Come by anytime! Hey, let me get your address, I'll send you some Dickie V stuff! I'll send you my new book! Hoops wrote it for me! I'll autograph it for you!"

Stevie started to say thank you and pull out his notebook to write down his address, but Vitale was off and running, jumping onto the podium. "Hey, give it to Hoops, okay, he'll get it to me! Great meeting you! Hoops, you're the best, baby! Check out that rumor; I'm telling you, it's the real deal!"

"So, how was that?" Weiss said as Vitale put his headset on and they turned back to the court, where the clock was now under a minute.

"Exhausting," Stevie said.

"He's actually kind of calm today," Weiss said. "Come on, I'll introduce you to Krzyzewski. You can tell him what a big fan you are."

Stevie laughed nervously. He had been at the Final Four for less than eight minutes and he was already feeling a little overwhelmed.

The buzzer sounded. The clock reset to fifty minutes and the Duke managers began grabbing balls and feeding them to the waiting players. He heard a cheer coming from a corner of the court where a group of Duke fans, dressed in blue and white, had gathered. He looked over and saw Krzyzewski walking out of the tunnel, dressed in sweats with a whistle around his neck.

"Showtime," Weiss said.

Behind him, Stevie could hear Vitale. "I am just PUMPED to be here in the Big Easy! Hey, it's Final Four Friday! It's gonna be AWESOME, BABEEE!!!!"

4: "STUDENT-ATHLETES"

WEISS AND STEVIE maneuvered through a sea of Minicams and still photographers who were milling around at the end of the court in the small area where they were allowed to be. An unsmiling NCAA official was standing there, warning them not to step over the line of tape that had been placed on the court as a stop sign.

"What happens if someone steps over the line?" Stevie asked Weiss.

"One of two things," Weiss said. "They either lose their credential or they're hung by their thumbs from the roof of the building."

Judging by the look on the NCAA guy's face, Stevie suspected Weiss wasn't joking.

They walked along press row—there were actually three

rows stretching the length of the court—in the direction of midcourt. Stevie could see that Krzyzewski was talking to Jim Nantz and Billy Packer of CBS, who were seated in what would undoubtedly be their seats the next day.

"The coaches have to spend a few minutes with the CBS guys," Weiss explained to Stevie as they walked up. "Most of them are like Mike; they get it over with early."

"Why do they have to?" Stevie asked.

Weiss laughed. "I can give you about a billion reasons why," he said. "As in, CBS is paying the NCAA a billion dollars for the TV rights and they want their announcers to be able to say 'When we talked to Coach K yesterday, he told us . . .'"

Stevie nodded his head. He *did* hear announcers talking about what the coaches had told them the day before a game, all the time. And Vitale was always talking about having lunch or dinner with them.

Several other people were standing around trying to listen in on the conversation between the famous coach and the famous TV people. Two of them, Stevie noticed, were Bill Brill and Susan Carol Anderson. As Stevie and Weiss walked up to the group, Krzyzewski excused himself from Nantz and Packer and walked a couple of steps to his right, to where Brill and Susan Carol were standing. Stevie could see he had a broad smile on his face as he approached them.

"Well, Brill, I see that the quality of reporter you're hanging around with has improved considerably," he said, shaking hands with Brill and then with Susan Carol.

"This is about as close as *I'll* ever get to being a writing-contest winner," Brill answered. "Being a tour guide for someone who can actually write."

Susan Carol was blushing. Stevie worried she might put a hand to her forehead and keel over in a dead faint when Krzyzewski said, "It's nice to see you again. Congratulations."

Brill apparently saw Weiss and Stevie coming, because he pointed to Stevie and said, "Here's our other contest winner now."

Stevie felt his stomach churn just a little as Krzyzewski, still smiling, turned to him and Weiss. "Hey, Hoops, how's it going?" he said, shaking hands with Weiss. He turned to Stevie, put out his hand, and said, "I read your story on the Palestra in the USBWA newsletter. It was terrific. I love that place."

Now it was Stevie's turn to feel a hot flash across his face. Oh God, he thought, I'm blushing like a girl! Ever since winning the contest, he had fantasized about going to Krzyzewski's press conference and being the only one in the room with the guts to stand up and say, "Coach, do you ever feel guilty about getting all the calls all the time?" Or "Coach, why do you think the referees let you get away with murder?" He knew Duke was good, but it seemed like the Blue Devils got all the breaks in close games.

He had envisioned the angry look on Krzyzewski's face, had pictured him saying, "Who asked that question?" and him standing to say, "My name is Steve Thomas and, unlike the rest of these guys, you can't intimidate me." He would be the talk of the Final Four, the kid who stood up to the mighty and evil Coach K.

Now the mighty and evil Coach K was standing a foot away from him, a friendly smile on his face, telling him how much he enjoyed his work. Stevie was searching for his voice, knew it had to be somewhere inside his throat, but couldn't find it. He finally managed to squeak, "Thanks, Coach."

Everyone seemed amused by his clear discomfort. Brill jumped in to help. "You know, Mike, Steven's a Big Five fan and a Big East guy. He's not a Duke fan at all."

"Why should he be?" Krzyzewski said. "When I was growing up in Chicago, I barely knew what the ACC was. I was a Big Ten guy all the way." He gave Stevie a friendly pat on the shoulder. "Don't let anyone tell you who to pull for." He paused. "Of course, I know when you actually *write* about us, you'll be fair, like all good reporters are. Right, Brill?"

Now everyone listening was having a good laugh. It was Susan Carol who jumped in at that point. "I think Mr. Brill is always fair," she said.

"Absolutely," Krzyzewski said. "So do I. Now, Roy Williams might have a different opinion. . . ."

"I get along just fine with Roy," said Brill, who had now joined the blush parade. "He's a good guy."

"For someone from Carolina," Krzyzewski said, as if finishing the sentence for him.

A whistle blew behind them. Krzyzewski shook hands all around again, saying to Stevie and Susan Carol, "You two have a great time this weekend. Watch these guys work, because, seriously, they're the best at what they do." Then he turned directly to Stevie. "And you come down and visit us at Duke sometime. Cameron's not as old as the Palestra, but it's pretty cool. Call my office and I'll set you up with seats right behind our bench. Anytime."

He turned to join his players, who were assembling in a circle at midcourt. Weiss put an arm around Stevie. "Really bad guy, huh?"

"Well, I mean . . . Do you think he's serious about those tickets?"

"Completely serious," Weiss said. "Come on, let's sit down and watch practice. You look like you need to catch your breath."

■ ■ ■

Stevie had never seen a college basketball team practice before. In fact, the only practices he had ever taken in were the ones he took part in at school and in summer camp. This was light-years different. In Stevie's practices at school there was one coach and ten players. Duke's practice had more people involved than Stevie could possibly keep track of. There were, by his count, fourteen players in the blue-and-white practice gear. Then there were a bunch of people in sweat suits like the one Krzyzewski was wearing. Three he recognized as assistant coaches Johnny Dawkins, Chris Collins, and Steve Wojciechowski. There were no fewer than twenty others roaming around the court, including one group who were clearly managers. Every time a player fell or anyone got tangled up, several of them would sprint to the spot as soon as play went to the other end of the court and feverishly towel up any sweat that might have dropped to the floor.

"Who *are* all these people?" Stevie asked Weiss, once they had settled into seats marked NEW YORK TIMES and CHICAGO TRIBUNE that were located not far from the CBS people. Stevie tried to picture himself actually sitting in one of those seats during a Final Four game and became dizzy at the notion.

"There are twelve managers," Weiss said. "They actually have to interview to get the job. The seniors interview freshmen and then pick them. It's a big honor."

"To wipe up sweat?"

"There's more to it than that. You get to be inside a great basketball program. The best coaches have had managers who go on to be coaches in a lot of cases. Lawrence Frank was a manager for Bob Knight at Indiana. K's had several managers become successful coaches, too."

Stevie was slightly amazed at the thought that Lawrence Frank, who coached the New Jersey Nets, had once wiped perspiration for basketball players at Indiana.

"The older guys are the team trainers and doctors and their sports information people," Weiss went on. "Big-time college basketball teams are a traveling circus. Today you've got a ringside seat."

No kidding, Stevie thought. He glanced around and saw TV crews eagerly taping the practice from different angles. Dawkins, who Stevie's dad had told him once played for the 76ers, thereby making him a good guy, was talking to someone who was scribbling notes as he spoke. In the corner, up on the little riser that was their set, Stevie could see the ESPN guys. Vitale was speaking and Digger Phelps and Chris Fowler were listening. Or perhaps, Stevie thought, not listening.

Stevie noticed that the scoreboard clock had just ticked under forty minutes. "Isn't fifty minutes kind of a short practice?" he asked.

"They're not really practicing here," Weiss said. "Watch, they won't do anything very serious. They'll all go practice someplace private later in the day once they get through with their press conferences."

Hearing Weiss mention the press conferences made Stevie remember that he still had to come up with a story before the end of the day. He glanced down at Susan Carol, sitting a few seats away, seemingly enthralled by the Duke practice. He was, he realized, very jealous of her. She had already written her story, so she could just sit back and enjoy the day.

"When's the first press conference?" he asked Weiss. "I need to come up with a story."

"As soon as Duke finishes. They go first, then the other three schools come in after them for thirty minutes at a time."

"Do the players go in to talk or just the coach?"

"Coach and two players. The other players have to stay in the locker room to be available during that same time period. Actually, you're probably better off in there than in the press conferences. You get pretty boring, generic 'We're just glad to be here' stuff in the press conferences. In the locker room, if you can find a guy who isn't a star who has a story to tell, you might get lucky."

Stevie's hope to write something about Chip Graber seemed unlikely now. Graber wasn't just the star of the Minnesota State team, he was the rock star of the team. He would certainly be one of the two Minnesota State players brought to the press conference, and each of the thousand reporters there that day would want to talk to him. "I guess writing about Chip Graber is out of the question," he said.

Weiss laughed. "Well, if you want to write the same story that every non-basketball columnist in America is going to write, you can write Chip Graber," he said.

"Non-basketball columnist?"

"The guys who don't cover basketball all year and then show up at the Final Four. Listen in the Minnesota State press conference. You'll know who they are. They'll be the guys who ask questions like 'Chip, what's it like to play for your dad?' As if he hasn't answered *that* question a couple thousand times since October. They're what we call 'event' guys. They come because this is an event, not because they know anything about basketball."

Stevie certainly didn't want to be an event guy. Especially at his first event.

"I think I'll write about someone else," he said.

"Good thinking," Weiss answered.

■ ■ ■

When the buzzer went off, signaling the end of Duke's time on the court, a lot of the writers and camerapeople who were courtside began making their way back under the stands. Krzyzewski and his players were waving at the cadre of Duke fans as they walked off; the managers were gathering up towels and water bottles in the players' wake. Weiss stood up, signaled Stevie to follow him, and they began walking toward the tunnel, where they were joined by Bill Brill and Susan Carol Anderson.

"Wasn't that great?" Susan Carol panted.

Stevie had to admit—to himself—that it had been pretty impressive. There must have been ten thousand people watching inside the massive Dome, and he had been sitting a few feet from the court watching a Final Four team practice. Even if Weiss insisted it wasn't a real practice, it had looked pretty real to him—especially the dunking contest the players had put on at the end.

"It was just a practice," he shrugged, trying to sound as casual as possible.

For the first time since they had met that morning, Susan Carol got a look on her face that indicated something other than complete pleasure. "I guess in Philadelphia you get to watch college teams practice all the time," she said, with a little bit of sarcasm in her voice, even though "time" came out of her mouth as "taam."

"No," he said, more defensively than he would have liked. "I'm just saying, it was only a *practice*."

"I've had coaches tell me that one of their great thrills is walking on the floor for Friday practice at the Final Four," Brill said. "There are practices and there are *practices*."

"And then there are *Coach K's* practices, right, Brill?" Weiss said.

"Well, yeah, of course," Brill answered, smiling.

They walked underneath the stands and followed signs directing them to the interview room. Like everything else he had seen so far, the interview room was about ten times larger than Stevie could possibly have imagined. The interview room in the Palestra was slightly larger than his bedroom at home. But this wasn't even really a room; it was a gigantic open area with blue curtains running down each side to give the impression of being a "room." It was longer than a football field, with giant TV monitors in several places around the room so that those in the back could see.

"Goodness," Susan Carol said when they walked in.

"Yeah," Stevie said, forgetting that he was being cool.

"Just like the Palestra, huh, Steve?" Weiss said.

Stevie grunted in response. Up front, a moderator was droning on about the schedule for the afternoon. No one from Duke had arrived yet.

"Once we get started," the moderator said, "we're going to take questions first for the student-athletes from Duke. The student-athletes will answer questions for fifteen minutes and then will return to the locker room. Once the student-athletes are dismissed, the coach will take questions for fifteen minutes. While he is answering questions, the student-athletes from his team will be available in the locker room to answer questions there. Please do *not* attempt to interview any of the student-athletes while they are in transit from the interview room to the locker room."

"I got four," Brill said.

"Think you missed one," Weiss said. "I had five."

"What are you guys talking about?" Stevie asked.

"'Student-athlete' references," Weiss said. "The moderator has strict marching orders from the NCAA to always refer to the players as 'student-athletes.' It's in the official handbook that they have to read beforehand. Most of the moderators are such puppets that they go crazy with the 'student-athlete' references. This guy is off to a flying start."

"Who is that guy?" Brill asked.

"I think it's Tim Schmink from the Hall of Fame. Apparently he gave a blood oath to say 'student-athletes' no fewer than a hunderd times before the end of the weekend."

"Only ninety-five to go," Susan Carol said, surprising Stevie. In five minutes she had shown a hint of sarcasm and now humor.

Krzyzewski was walking onto the podium, followed by two of his players, J.J. Redick and Shelden Williams.

"Okay," Tim Schmink said. "We're now ready. Coach Krzyzewski is here with student-athletes J.J. Redick and Shelden Williams. We'll take questions for the student-athletes first."

"Ninety-three," Stevie and Susan Carol said together.

They both laughed. Damn, Stevie thought, she's really kind of pretty. He wasn't pleased with himself for thinking that.

5: ROAMING THE HALLS

SIX "STUDENT-ATHLETE" REFERENCES and fifteen minutes later, the Duke student-athletes were dismissed. Each had used the phrase "step up" twice. Both were really happy to be here and Redick vowed to give "a hundred and ten percent." Stevie remembered reading a funny column somewhere pointing out that giving more than one hundred percent was, in fact, impossible. He was tempted to steal the line, but Susan Carol had such a dreamy look on her face that he decided to skip the wisecrack.

Stevie was getting restless by the time Redick and Williams left. But Krzyzewski was, he had to admit, more interesting. There were no references to stepping up or giving a hundred and ten percent. Clearly, Krzyzewski had done this a few times. He even called his student-athletes players. Stevie wondered if that might be more than the moderator could bear.

St. Joe's came in next. Glancing at a printed schedule that he had picked up out on press row, Stevie could see how the system worked. Since UConn was on the court between 1:00 and 2:00, St. Joe's came into the interview room at 1:30. UConn would come in at 2:00, when its practice was over, and St. Joe's would take the court. Minnesota State would come in to be interviewed at 2:30, before its 3:00 practice.

The St. Joe's press conference wasn't much different than Duke's. The official "student-athlete" count soared to twenty-one by the time the Hawks players left for their locker room. Phil Martelli, the coach, filled a lot of notebooks with one-liners. By the time UConn came into the room, Stevie was getting seriously antsy. Weiss had clearly been right—nothing terribly interesting was going to come out of these press conferences. As Jim Calhoun and his players were sitting down and the moderator was giving his "student-athletes" speech *again*, Stevie decided his first story idea was probably his best bet: a day in the life of a kid reporter at the Final Four. He could write about Vitale and Krzyzewski and even Big Tex. He'd get a final tally on the number of "student-athlete" references—now at twenty-six as the questioning of the UConn players began. He needed to get out of here, though, and see what the scene looked like in the locker rooms and around the rest of the building. What he most wanted to do was see what it was like to be Chip Graber, even if it meant standing on the outside of the circle while people tried to talk to him in the locker room after his fifteen minutes in the interview room.

"I think I'll go for a walk around the building," he said to Weiss, who was scribbling notes while Rashad Anderson was talking. "I want to check out the locker rooms."

"You okay on your own?" Weiss asked.

"Sure. As long as I have my pass, I can get wherever I need to go, right?"

Weiss nodded. "I'll be here until Minnesota State is finished. Then I'll be back in the working area."

"Okay, I'll meet you there."

Stevie stood up.

"Can I go with you?"

Surprised, Stevie saw Susan Carol standing up, too (he'd been a lot more comfortable sitting next to her than standing next to her), with a shy smile on her face.

Stevie had been about to ask her to get him a final count on the "student-athlete" references. "Um, well, yeah, sure, I guess. I was going to try to find something to write about, and you're already done. I was hoping you might keep track of how many times the guy says 'student-athletes' between now and the end of the last press conference for me."

"What's the count now?" Weiss said.

"Twenty-six," they both answered. Stevie had to admit he was impressed that she'd been keeping track, too.

"I'll do it for you," Weiss said. "In fact, it might make a funny little note."

"So, it's okay then?" Susan Carol said.

"Yeah, sure," Stevie said. "But let's go. I want to see some of the place and then be in the Minnesota State locker room at two forty-five when they bring Graber back in from here."

"You'll never get close to him," Weiss said.

"That's fine. I don't need to get close."

Weiss gave him a funny look, but Stevie decided there wasn't time to explain. Once they were out in the hallway, Susan Carol said, "This is a good idea—I was bored to death in there."

"You didn't look bored when Coach K was talking."

"What exactly is your problem with Coach K?" she said. "He's a great coach, and you just saw what kind of person he is. You know, if you're going to be a reporter, you're going to have to put your biases aside."

"What about *your* biases?" Stevie shot back, relieved that she had given him an opening. "You don't think he can do anything wrong. That's just as much a bias as mine."

"You're right," she said. "But if he ever did something wrong, I think I'd be disappointed, but I'd admit he was wrong."

"Has he *ever* done anything wrong?" Stevie asked.

She thought about that one for a minute. "Well," she finally said, "he *is* a Republican."

"I thought everyone from the South was a Republican."

"Oh yes, and we're all good ole boys and Southern belles, too. I do declare, Steven Thomas, you are just full of misconceptions." Susan Carol's voice was dripping drawl.

This girl was really starting to get on his nerves. Mostly because she was right so often.

"Well, how lucky I am to have you to correct me then."

They had now reached the hallway that led to the locker rooms. There were signs directing people to the four team locker rooms and to just about every other place one might want to go. There was also a security guard very carefully checking credentials as people approached the hallway. The guard glanced at Susan Carol's pass, nodded at her, and then put up a hand to stop Stevie.

"Whoa, fella, this area's restricted. Working media only."

Stevie looked down at the credential dangling around his neck. It was no different from the one Susan Carol was wearing or, for that matter, the ones that Dick Weiss and Bill Brill and all the other writers had been wearing. It had his name on it and "USBWA" and "media." It was, he thought, pretty clear-cut.

"I *am* working media," Stevie said, pointing to the word on his credential and attempting to step around the guard so he could get this over with sooner rather than later. Susan Carol, a few steps ahead, had stopped and turned around to see what was going on.

"Look, son, I don't know where you got that pass or how, but if you don't turn around and walk back in the other direction right now, I'll put in a call to security and then whatever little game you're playing will be over for the day. So get going."

Stevie felt himself flush with anger. His first thought was to ask why the guard had let Susan Carol pass and not him, but the answer was obvious: He looked thirteen; she could easily pass for eighteen. Before he could say something he would undoubtedly regret, Susan Carol stepped up next to the guard and said, "Sir, I understand your confusion. But we're both winners of the USBWA student writing contest." She opened her notebook and pulled out a piece of paper that Stevie recognized as the letter informing them that they had won the contest.

"Here's the letter we got from the USBWA," she said. "You see the two names? I'm Susan Carol Anderson and he's Steven Thomas. You see what the letter says: that we'll be fully accredited media at the Final Four."

The guard looked at the letter—Stevie was relieved when it became apparent that he knew how to read—then looked at the names on their credentials. He looked at Susan Carol again. "So you two are in high school then?" he said.

"Junior high school," Susan Carol said, smiling. Clearly this wasn't the first time someone had mistaken her for older than thirteen. "We're both eighth graders."

The guard was clearly put out by the whole thing. He handed the letter back to Susan Carol. "Okay, if they want to give passes to eighth graders, that's their call. You can go on ahead." He looked Stevie over again. "But don't get in anyone's way back there, understand?"

"I think 'I'm really sorry for accusing you of stealing' was what you meant to say."

"Listen, kid, don't get smart with me. I can throw you out of here, pass or no pass," the guard said.

Stevie was about to say something about the need for *one* of them to be smart, when Susan Carol grabbed him by the arm, practically shoving him in front of her and away from the glowering guard. "Thanks for your help," she said, then gave Stevie an extra push to make sure he didn't try to get in a final verbal swipe. Stevie stumbled but regained his balance before falling.

"What was that about?" he said as she pulled up even with him, one hand on his back to keep him moving forward.

"That was about avoiding trouble," she hissed. "Is it a guy thing or a Northern thing to always have to have the last word? He's letting us by. If he wants to say something to make himself feel better, just let him say it."

"Easy for you to say—you're not the one he stopped."

"No, I'm not. I'm the one who got you past him without a big scene."

She had him there.

"Why are you carrying that letter around?"

"Because I thought something like that might happen. That someone would look at me and think I'm too young to be a real reporter."

Stevie laughed. "Apparently that wasn't a problem, was it?"

She blushed a little, which pleased him. "Yeah, for once being tall worked for me. Turns out it was a good thing I had the letter, though, right?"

"Yeah, right."

Stevie was glad no one was keeping score on their exchanges, because he had the sense he was in a deep hole.

The hallway was crowded. The first locker room they

came to was marked SAINT JOE'S. There were several more guards milling around outside the door, which was open. Stevie was convinced they were all eyeing him suspiciously. He leaned around one of them to look into the locker room and saw it was empty. That made sense, since the Hawks were on the court practicing. Stevie felt slightly guilty that he wasn't out there watching *his* team, but he had work to do. He glanced at his watch: it was 2:12. That meant he had about thirty minutes to scope the place out before the Chip Graber circus began.

The Duke locker room, which they came to next, was just as empty as Saint Joe's. The Blue Devils had left the building, their practice and press conferences long over. Most of the action was outside the Connecticut locker room. As a Big East fan, Stevie knew that UConn was covered by more reporters on a regular basis than any team in the country. The UConn media was known as "the Horde."

As Stevie and Susan Carol walked up, they could see someone being interviewed outside the locker-room door who wasn't a player. He looked to Stevie like a coach but he knew Jim Calhoun was still in the interview room.

"Who is that?" he asked Susan Carol.

She shook her head, then tapped one of the reporters standing on the outside of the circle and said, "Excuse me, sir, who are you fellas interviewing?"

The reporter looked over his shoulder and said softly, "George Blaney."

"Who's that?" Stevie said.

The reporter looked at him as if he was a kid who didn't

know anything—which, apparently, he was. "He's the number one assistant," he hissed, then returned to listening intently to what Blaney was saying.

"Whoo boy," Stevie said to Susan Carol. "These guys must be pretty desperate, fighting to get a quote from an assistant."

"At Duke, Johnny Dawkins gets interviewed all the time," she said.

"Yeah, like I said," Stevie said. "What do Duke and UConn have in common?"

"Great basketball teams?"

"And they're both in places that don't have pro teams, so they're the only game in town for the media."

She shook her head the way his mother sometimes did when he was being obtuse. "There are three pro teams in North Carolina," she said. "Hockey, football, basketball. Plus, the University of North Carolina is bigger than Duke in the media there because most people in the state are Carolina fans. Duke isn't even *close* to being the only game in town. I'm sure you think that Philadelphia is the world's greatest sports town, but North Carolina isn't exactly Nowheresville."

Stevie sighed. "I stand corrected—again."

She smiled. "You want to go in here and try to talk to some of the players?"

Stevie wasn't sure. He was thinking he could write about the Horde and their quest for quotes from George Blaney as part of his story, but he didn't need a quote for that. He spotted a sign on the wall that said MINNESOTA STATE LOCKER

ROOM with an arrow pointing farther down the hallway and CBS COMPOUND with an arrow pointing in the same direction. That gave Stevie an idea.

"Let's walk down here," he said. "I want to end up in the Minnesota State locker room, but we can explore down this way first."

Susan Carol shrugged. "What exactly are you looking for?"

"Don't know," Stevie said. "Just trying to find something no one else is going to have. I don't think I'm going to find anything like that around here."

She nodded in agreement and they started down the hall. There was no one around the Minnesota State locker room except for—of course—the usual gaggle of security people and a man wearing a suit sitting in a golf cart. He was carrying a walkie-talkie.

"Team not here yet?" Stevie asked the guy in the golf cart.

"Any minute," he answered pleasantly. "We just got word their bus is pulling into the parking lot."

Stevie noticed the credential dangling around his neck. It had a big "AA" on it, and "All Access" under that in case there was any doubt about what it meant.

"Do you work for the NCAA?" Stevie asked.

The man laughed. "Hardly. My name's Roger Valdiserri. I used to be the SID at Notre Dame. I'm just helping out with the media this weekend."

He had a friendly smile and he put out his hand as he introduced himself.

"I'm Stevie Thomas," Stevie said, forgetting that he was supposed to be Steve in the adult world. "This is Susan Carol Anderson."

"Oh yes," Roger Valdiserri said. "You're the contest winners. I read about you guys. Congratulations. You having fun?"

They both nodded. "What's the golf cart for?" Stevie asked.

"As soon as Coach Graber gets here, I pop him and his two players on here"—he reached out to pat the two seats in the back that faced away from the driver—"and get them down to the interview room. You guys might have noticed it's a pretty good walk from here."

"So Chip Graber will be riding on your golf cart in a few minutes?" Susan Carol asked.

"I would assume he'll be one of the two players going to the interview room," Valdiserri said. "You want me to try to get you an autograph?"

Susan Carol stood up very straight as if she had just been insulted. "Of course not," she said. "We're here as reporters."

Valdiserri smiled. "Good for you, honey."

"Do you think we can walk down to the CBS compound?" Stevie asked.

"I don't see why not," Valdiserri said. "They let the TV writers down there and you guys have media passes. If you have any trouble, let me know and I'll see what I can do."

They thanked him, shook hands again, and continued down the hall. There were two large double doors at the end of it and, much to Stevie's surprise, no security people to stop them. They walked up to the doors, pushed them open, and peered around. It was relatively dark on the other side of the doors. It looked to Stevie as if they were on some kind of a loading dock. To their left, he could see what he guessed would normally be space that was part of the football field. There were several giant trucks with the CBS logo on the side and a small city of trailers. Everywhere Stevie looked, there were people scurrying in different directions, in and out of the trailers and the trucks. There were steps at the end of the loading dock that led down to the CBS compound, and, as Stevie and Susan Carol stood taking it all in, two young men came bounding up the steps carrying walkie-talkies.

"The bus just pulled up," Stevie heard one of them say. "Is there a crew there? We'll get people to the entrance hallway in about thirty seconds."

"Sounds like the Purple Tide has arrived," Stevie said to Susan Carol as the two CBS types swept past them and through the double doors without so much as a glance in their direction. Roger Valdiserri had been right. Apparently the CBS people didn't care if anyone from the media walked into their compound. And anyone who made it into their compound another way was obviously cleared to go through the double doors to the locker room hallway. Thus the surprising absence of security people. Stevie had been beginning to think even the bathrooms would have security guards.

"You want to walk down there and see if there's anyone

interesting from CBS to talk to?" Susan Carol asked.

"Maybe," Stevie said. He was looking to his right, where there was a shard of light coming from the other end of the loading dock. "I wonder what's over there."

"Nothing probably," Susan Carol said.

"Let's take a quick look."

He led her toward the spot where the light was coming from. There was a lot of stuff stored here, piled up on the back end of the dock. The light came from a back entrance to the Dome that was about twenty yards from the loading dock.

"Nothing here," Susan Carol said. "I guess we—" She stopped in mid-sentence. "Hey, look who's here."

She pointed across the dark, open area to the outside door. Stevie could see a group of young men in purple-and-white sweats coming through the doorway. "Straight down this hall to the end and turn right, gentlemen," someone they couldn't see was saying. "Your locker room is the first one you come to on your right."

"As if they can't read the signs," Stevie said.

"He must have forgotten that they're student-athletes," Susan Carol said.

Stevie laughed. He hated to admit it, but she *was* kind of funny.

"Well," she said. "Should we head—"

She stopped in mid-sentence again. Stevie turned and saw one final purple-and-white-suited player walk through the doorway, peering around as if to make sure no one was there. Stevie recognized the floppy blond hair right away. It was Chip Graber. Right behind him was a man in a charcoal gray suit who was also looking around in a suspicious way. Instinctively, Stevie took Susan Carol's arm and stepped back so they were hidden behind some rolled-up Astroturf.

Graber and the charcoal suit finally seemed satisfied they were alone, then walked toward the loading dock until they were almost directly below Stevie and Susan Carol—who were both frozen with surprise and curiosity.

"Okay, Chip, we've got about two minutes to get this straight before the press conference," the suit said. "You can't get cold feet now."

"I never had *warm* feet," Chip Graber answered in a stage whisper, still plenty loud enough for Stevie and Susan Carol to hear. "What if I won't do it?"

"Then the team gets stripped of all its wins and your father gets fired. We've been through this. . . ."

There was a long silence. Stevie wondered if perhaps the conversation had ended, but there were no signs of movement below. Susan Carol started to open her mouth to say something, but he put a finger to his lips to indicate she should stay silent.

Just when Stevie thought he was wrong, he heard Graber's voice again. "This is unbelievable."

"Hey, Chip, the world's a cold place sometimes. Cooperate and you'll be a millionaire in a couple of months. Your dad will get a big contract extension for making the Final Four. Quit whining, do what you need to do, and we'll all walk away happy."

"But what if we lose Saturday? There's no guarantee we'll

win that game. Why does it have to be Monday?"

"That's not something you need to worry about. You just play your butt off against St. Joe's and choke against Duke. We'll take care of the rest."

"I'll get you for this. All of you."

"Please. You don't even know who *we* are. And if you try anything with me, the roof will fall in on you and your dad. Now let's go. You've got a press conference."

This time they could hear footsteps walking away. Stevie and Susan Carol stood stock-still for a moment looking at one another.

"What did we just hear?" she asked finally.

"Well, unless I'm crazy, we just heard the best player in the country being blackmailed to throw the championship game."

"Yeah, that's what I heard, too. But he has to win tomorrow. Isn't that weird? I don't know very much about gambling, but if someone is trying to make a lot of money by betting against Minnesota State, why wait until Monday?"

"That's what Graber asked. There's got to be a reason why it has to be Monday. And he said he had to lose to *Duke* on Monday. How's he know Duke will win tomorrow?"

For the first time since they had met that morning, Stevie thought Susan Carol looked lost. "What do we do?" she asked.

Stevie shook his head. "I don't know. Tell someone?"

"But who?" she asked. "Who'd believe us?"

"Good question," he said. "I barely believe us. Man, I

wanted a story no one else had, but this is insane. Let's get out of here. It's spooky."

She didn't argue.

As they opened the doors that led back to the hallway and the bright lights hit Stevie's eyes, he felt like he was leaving a movie. But there was no leaving. Now he and Susan Carol were *part* of the movie.

6: WHAT NOW?

THEY HADN'T GONE VERY FAR back down the locker room hall-way when they were stopped by a gaggle of security people. Stevie looked intently for the guy in the charcoal gray suit, wanting to get a better look at his face, but he didn't see him.

Someone with a walkie-talkie faced the assembled media and announced that the locker room would be open in three minutes, "at precisely two-thirty. Student-athletes will be available for thirty minutes after that."

"Does that count?" Susan Carol asked.

"Huh?"

"In the 'student-athlete' count."

His story! How was he supposed to write a "Gee, isn't it cool to be here" story when they'd just stumbled onto the scandal of the year?

"I nearly forgot—I still have to write a story," he told Susan Carol.

"But what about Graber and that man?" she asked.

"Listen, neither one of us is sure what we just heard or what we should do about it," he said. "How about giving me an hour to write something and then we can decide what to do next?"

She nodded. "Okay. But don't you need to wait for Graber to come back here from the interview room?"

"I don't want to take the time. I'll just write about meeting Vitale and K and the security guard and the 'student-athletes.' I think I can fill eight hundred words with that stuff pretty quickly."

"Can you really do that in an hour?"

Stevie nodded. Once he had a story in his head, the words seemed to gush out of him when he sat down at a computer. If he could keep himself focused on something other than Chip Graber for the next hour, he could easily finish the story.

"I'm going to go back to the workroom and get this done," he said.

"Okay," she said. "I'll go back on the court, find a quiet place to sit, and try to write down as much of what we heard as I can remember."

Again, Stevie had to admit she was smart. "Yeah, good idea," he said. "And keep an eye out for the man in the gray suit. But don't say a word to anyone because—"

She cut him off with a look that said, *Don't tell me what I already know.*

"Sorry," he said. "I'm just nervous."

"I'm not," she said. "I'm scared."

Once again, she was a step ahead of him.

■ ■ ■

Stevie followed the signs back to the media workroom, still amazed by how many people there were in the bowels of the massive building. It took him a minute to re-create in his mind where he and Weiss had walked to when they first came into the room a few hours earlier, but he finally found their computers side by side near a sign that said NEW YORK DAILY NEWS. He crawled under the table to plug in his computer, turned it on, and began writing. He was so pumped up with adrenaline that he didn't even hear Weiss when he came in and sat down next to him.

"Looks like you're rolling," Weiss said.

Stevie glanced up, realized Weiss was talking to him, and said cleverly, "Whaa?"

"I said you're rolling," Weiss repeated.

"Oh yeah, well, I figured I'd better get going."

"Good thought. When you finish, I'll help you file it if you need. Did you write about Graber?"

Stevie almost gagged. "What?! Oh, um, no, it was just a zoo in there. Did he say anything in the press conference?"

"That he was really proud to play for his dad. He was actually pretty quiet. He's usually more outgoing. I guess he's human, feeling the pressure."

"Yeah, pressure," Stevie said, thinking, You don't know the half of it.

"By the way, the final 'student-athlete' count was thirty-nine," Weiss said.

"I'll make it forty," Stevie said. "I heard one more outside the Minnesota State locker room."

Weiss laughed. "Good for you."

He settled down to work while Stevie finished his story. Stevie wasn't terribly proud of what he produced. He knew he had rushed and he hadn't done nearly as much work on the story as he had planned. But all of his plans for the weekend had changed in those few minutes he and Susan Carol spent on the loading dock. Weiss volunteered to read the story for him before he filed it. Stevie really didn't want to waste any more time, but he couldn't turn down Weiss's offer without being rude. Fortunately, Weiss didn't take too long to read it.

"It's good," he said. "I like what you said about Dickie V, 'a one-man twenty-four-hour sports-talk radio station.' That's clever."

"Thanks," Stevie said. "I think I'm ready to send."

Weiss helped him get online and Stevie tapped in the e-mail address for the editor who would edit his story and send it out to the other papers that were using his and Susan Carol's features. He attached the story, hit the send button, and was relieved when the computer told him his mail had been sent successfully. He called the number he had been given for the editor.

"Tom Vernon," a voice said after the first ring.

"Mr. Vernon?" Stevie said. "This is Steve Thomas at the Final Four." He paused for a moment, thinking how cool that sounded. "I just sent you my story."

"Oh, Steve, that's great," Tom Vernon said. "Call me Tom. Let me see if it's here." Stevie heard him tapping some computer buttons. "Got it," he said. "Little long, but we'll work with it."

Stevie was surprised that he had written too much, but then he'd been pretty fired up while he was writing, thinking about what he and Susan Carol had to do once he was finished, and not about the word count of his story.

"Sorry," Stevie said.

"No problem, just some good spadework. Do me a favor and call me back in an hour or so in case I have questions. Okay?"

"Sure, yeah," Stevie said. "Thanks."

He hung up the phone and turned to Weiss. "What's good spadework?" he asked.

Weiss smiled. "It means you did a lot of digging," he said. "You know, as in digging up a good story."

Stevie liked that. An inside journalism term. But now, he thought, the real spadework was about to begin.

■ ■ ■

Susan Carol was in the third row of the press seating area taking notes while the last ten minutes of Minnesota State's practice were winding down. She looked surprised when Stevie sat down next to her.

"Done already?" she said.

"Yeah," he said casually. "Mr. Vernon said I wrote a little long but he seemed to think I had done some good spadework."

She smiled. "Well, we've got some *real* spadework to do now, don't we?"

Stevie was deflated. Of course she knew what spadework was—this girl knew everything.

"I've written down as much as I can remember," she said. "Can you read it and see if I've got it right? I've been watching Graber during practice. I can't say he looks like anything's wrong. When he came out, there was all this squealing from the girls and he smiled and waved to them."

"Any sign of the guy in the gray suit?"

Susan Carol pointed across the court to one of the benches. "He's right there," she said. "Except there are two of him."

Stevie looked at the end of the bench and almost choked. There were two men sitting side by side in almost identical charcoal gray suits. Both had gray hair, the other feature Stevie had been able to pick up during the brief moment when the suit and Graber hadn't been in darkness.

She held up what looked like a purple-and-white magazine. It was the Minnesota State media guide, which contained photos of every person connected to the Minnesota State basketball team. "I've looked through this thing," she said. "There are at least six people who could be him. I've circled their pictures but I don't think we're going to figure out who it is from just looking."

"We need to hear the guy talk," Stevie said.

"Exactly—who could forget that voice? But how?" Talking to either gray suit was going to be a problem. They were sitting in the off-limits bench area.

Stevie thought for a minute. He glanced up at the score-board and saw the clock had just gone under eight minutes. Minnesota State would be leaving the court and the build-ing in under eight minutes, and they wouldn't really have a clue as to who Graber's blackmailer was.

"I've got an idea," he said. "Come with me, quick."

For once she didn't challenge him or ask any questions. The two of them walked down to the front row and toward the baseline. The number of writers, photographers, and cameramen had diminished considerably since the start of the Duke practice. Most writers were inside working on their stories, and the cameramen and photogs had the pic-tures they needed. Stevie and Susan Carol crossed to the bench side of the court.

They stopped a few paces shy of the corner of the court. There was—of course—a security guard posted there to pre-vent anyone from walking directly behind the bench. "Okay, here's what you're doing," Stevie said.

"What *I'm* doing?" she said.

"Yes, you," he said. "I want you to walk over to that secu-rity guard, give him the wide-eyed-Southern-girl routine, and tell him you really need to talk to your 'uncle' over there on the MSU bench."

"Wide-eyed-Southern-girl routine—what is that sup-posed to mean?"

"You know."

"No, I don't know and—"

"Yell at me later, would you?" he broke in. "We've got less than five minutes here. Just . . . be yourself. Smile.

Drawl. Say, 'Aah need to see mah uncle, kind suh.'"

"Who do you think I am, Scarlett O'Hara?" she said.

But before he could open his mouth, she had walked past him and was giving the security guard a smile that would have melted Rhett Butler. She was pointing at the gray-suit twins on the bench and looking just a bit distressed. It took less than thirty seconds for the security guard to step aside and let her pass.

Not wanting to be caught staring, Stevie stepped back a bit, moving toward the basket. As he did, he sensed a body flying in his direction and looked up just in time to duck out of the way of Chip Graber, who was racing after a loose ball. The Purple Tide was wrapping up its practice with a brief scrimmage, mostly for the entertainment of the fans, but Stevie's attention had been focused on the sidelines.

"Watch yourself, kid, you'll get hurt," Graber said as he turned to run downcourt. He gave Stevie a friendly smile, which made Stevie feel both better about being in the way and worse about Graber's predicament. He turned back to the bench area and saw one of the gray-suit twins pointing in the direction of the locker room as if giving Susan Carol directions. Stevie couldn't help but smile because he knew she was getting exactly what they needed.

She wrapped up her conversation and walked back to the baseline, pausing briefly to thank the security guard, who actually smiled at her.

"Well?" Stevie hissed impatiently.

"Hang on, walk into the tunnel," she said, nodding her head in the direction of the exit.

They walked up the ramp, turned the corner, and found a quiet spot. The place was now almost empty, with the last practice of the day about to end and all the press conferences complete. "I know which guy it is," she said. "Where's that MSU media guide? I can pick him out now. It was the one sitting closer to midcourt."

"I don't have the guide; we must have left it. You couldn't get a name off his credential?"

She shook her head. "No. He had it kind of stuffed in his pocket. He was wearing one of those pins they give the people with the teams, so he didn't need to have it out. We can't go back in there. I guess we'll have to get another media guide in the press room."

"What did you say to get them to talk?"

"I told them that I'd left my notebook sitting on a stool in their locker room and asked if someone could either get me in there to look or look for me. Our guy said a couple of their managers would still be in there and could help."

"Are you *sure* that he's our guy?"

She nodded. "Absolutely. The other guy had a much higher voice than the blackmailer. There was no mistaking it, really."

Stevie remembered that, even speaking in a hushed tone, Graber's blackmailer had a deep baritone voice.

"Nice going, Scarlett," he said as they headed for the press room.

"Oh, shut up, you wise-guy Yankee," she said, smiling in spite of herself.

The press room was alive with activity, since almost

everyone was writing now. Stevie could hear a number of radio guys doing reports, which he figured had to be very distracting for those trying to concentrate on writing. There was a table in the middle of the room piled high with media guides and postseason guides for the four teams. They grabbed one off the MSU pile and found an empty spot. They began paging through the book, but it didn't take long for Susan Carol to stab a picture and semi-shriek, "That's him!"

They were at the very front of the media guide, page 7 of a book that stretched on for 286 pages. Up front was a two-page bio of MSU president Earl A. Koheen. Then came Provost Hall Yantos and another man who no doubt had played a key role in the Purple Tide's success: Blake Arbutus, the chairman of the school's board of trustees. And next was Thomas R. Whiting, MSU's athletic department faculty representative . . . and resident blackmailer.

Stevie looked closely at the picture. She was right, Whiting was definitely the guy sitting on the bench nearer midcourt. A further search through the guide revealed that the man sitting next to him was team doctor Philip Katz. They looked closely at Whiting's biography: "Now in his twelfth year as MSU's faculty representative, Professor Thomas R. Whiting has worked closely during his tenure with administrators, coaches, and student-athletes to ensure that they are given the best possible opportunity to compete while enjoying both their athletic and academic experiences at MSU. Prior to his arrival at the Rochester campus, Professor Whiting taught at the University of Florida, the

University of Delaware, and his alma mater, Providence College, where one of his students was current MSU president Earl A. Koheen." The rest was just as boring, citing awards Whiting had received and committees he had served on, including, it said, the prestigious and important "NCAA subcommittee on gambling."

Stevie almost laughed out loud when he saw that. But Susan Carol was a step ahead of him. "Read the last line," she said. "Tell me if it doesn't make you sick."

Stevie scanned down to the last line: "Professor Whiting has been at MSU for the past eighteen years as a tenured professor in the political science department. He is best known for the senior seminar he teaches each fall: Ethics and Morals in American Society Today."

7: PLANNING AND PLOTTING

SO THEY KNEW who the bad guy was. Or at least one of the bad guys. Susan Carol was now officially angry. "A professor of ethics!" she railed, a little bit louder than Stevie would have liked, once they had closed the media guide. "That's disgusting."

"You mean it wouldn't be disgusting if it was the team doctor or someone else?" Stevie asked.

"Of course it would be disgusting," she said. "But if students can't trust their teachers, who can they trust? If you read the bio, you would think that this guy is a saint, a do-gooder."

"And if you read the player bios, you would think they're all student-athletes," Stevie said.

She smiled ruefully. "It's easier to be a fan when you watch on TV."

There was no arguing with that. Stevie had wanted the inside view of college ball, but he wasn't liking what he saw. Almost no one was who they appeared to be—or who the people running the event wanted you to think they were. The moderator kept screaming about "student-athletes," as if that would somehow make it true. Thomas R. Whiting, noted professor of ethics and morals in American society, had clearly lost track of his ethics and morals somewhere along the way. Stevie wondered if Chip Graber was really what he appeared to be. He'd kind of assumed that Graber was a victim—but maybe he'd done something really bad and was trying to cover it up.

"Who *can* we trust?" Susan Carol said as if she was reading his mind.

"And what do we do now?" Stevie said.

She thought about that for a minute. "I think we need help. Mr. Weiss or Mr. Brill? One of the NCAA people?"

Stevie laughed at that one. "You mean the people who are obsessed with convincing us that all the players are 'student-athletes'? I don't think they're going to be a lot of help."

"Cynical," she said. "But true."

"I suppose we could wait and see what happens in the games tomorrow," he said. "If Minnesota State loses, maybe it's over."

"All bets are off," she said, smiling.

"Funny," he said. "But Whiting did kind of threaten Graber if MSU loses."

"Which means we probably should tell *somebody*," she

said. "I think Mr. Weiss and Mr. Brill are our best chance."

Quickly reviewing their options again, Stevie realized she was right. He could see Brill packing up his computer. "Okay," he said. "Let's give it a shot."

They asked Brill if he had a minute to talk. He looked puzzled but said, "Sure," and the three of them walked over to where Weiss was working. He looked up and said, "Everyone finished but me, I guess."

"As usual, Hoops," Brill said. "The kids have something they want to ask us."

Weiss pushed back from his computer. "Believe it or not, I'm just about done. What's up, guys?"

Stevie glanced at Susan Carol. How to begin?

She sat down next to Weiss. "Has anyone ever tried to fix a game at the Final Four?" Susan Carol asked, her voice barely more than a whisper.

Weiss smiled. "A fix?" he said. "No. There's been point shaving through the years. I think the last time was Tulane in '85, right, Bill? But outright fixing? No. Especially nowadays, when the players all think they're going to be millionaires in the pros soon. Why do you ask?"

Susan Carol glanced at Stevie, who nodded for her to continue. "We think someone may be trying to blackmail a player."

"What in the world makes you think that?" Weiss said, looking perplexed.

"We overheard something," Stevie said. "A conversation."

"What'd they say?" Brill asked.

"Well, he said the player had to win tomorrow and then choke on Monday."

"Or else what?" said Brill.

"Um . . . I'm not sure exactly," said Susan Carol, looking to Stevie for help.

"He said that the team would forfeit all its wins and that the coach would be fired. But he didn't say why, or how . . . ," said Stevie, feeling suddenly unsure. This was sounding lame, even to him.

"Look, kids," Brill said, "I don't know what you heard, but my guess is you misunderstood. Hoops is right. There's a lot wrong with college basketball, but game fixing may be the one thing I really *don't* worry about. Any player who actually *could* fix a game at this level would be risking millions to do it."

Brill saw how serious the kids looked and backtracked a little. "If you can tell us more, we can try and check it out, though."

Stevie made a snap decision. "No, you're probably right," he said. "We only heard half the conversation."

"Yeah," Susan Carol said. "We'll see if we can find out any more and let you know if we do."

"Good idea," Hoops said. "Never hurts to keep your eyes and ears open.

"You know, if you want to hear about a real scandal, you should ask Bobby Kelleher about Brickley Shoes. Remember, Bill? Bobby caught that sneaker-company rep working behind the scenes for . . . Louisiana, wasn't it?"

"Yeah, that's right," said Brill. "There's plenty of dirt to be found in basketball. But no need to hear every rotten story in one weekend. There are plenty of good stories, too."

"Mmm. Speaking of which, I should finish this story," said Weiss.

"And I have to go do a radio show," Brill said. "Do you kids want to wait?"

Susan Carol shook her head. "We can get back to the hotel. It's just a short walk."

"You need anything, you'll call me, right, Steve?" Weiss asked.

Stevie nodded. Which reminded him: he hadn't called Mr. Vernon to check on his story.

"Are you sure you're thirteen?" the editor asked when Stevie reached him. "This is very well done." Stevie would have glowed with pride at the compliment if his mind hadn't been filled with a thousand other things.

He and Susan Carol packed up their stuff and headed out of the press room.

"What now?" she said, once they were back in the hallway. "You don't really think we misheard Graber and Whiting, do you?"

"No. And we *didn't* come in during the conversation, we heard the whole thing. I just said that because I knew they weren't going to believe us anyway. But I have to admit, it *doesn't* make any sense."

"The only thing I know is that the whole thing is sickening. They can't get away with it."

"Which is why, somehow, someway, we have to stop it,"

he said. "And," he added, "it looks like we're going to have to do it ourselves."

■ ■ ■

As they walked back across the bridge to the hotel, Stevie glanced at his watch. It was almost five o'clock. He had told his dad he would be back in the room by six, so he had some extra time.

"So, what's our next move?" Susan Carol asked as they walked into a surprisingly empty lobby.

Stevie tried to think. "You still have those notes you made while I was writing?" he said.

"Uh-huh, in my notebook."

"Okay. Let's sit down for a minute and go over what we know for sure. Then we can work on what we need to know and how to find out."

She smiled. "Mr. Vernon's right: you *are* good for thirteen."

He wasn't sure if she was teasing him for telling her what the editor had said or being serious. Either way, he pointed her to two chairs in the lobby, and she pulled out her notebook.

"All right," she said. "Begin at the beginning. The MSU faculty rep is blackmailing MSU's star player. We're pretty certain he isn't working alone."

"And we know he doesn't want tomorrow's game thrown," Stevie said. "It has to be Monday."

"Preferably against Duke," she added.

"Could Whiting be working for Duke?" he said.

She looked pained at the thought. "Worth writing down as a possibility," she said.

"Okay. What we *don't* know is what they've got on Graber. What could he have done that would mean his team would forfeit games and his dad would get fired?"

"Cheat somehow?" speculated Susan Carol.

"Maybe," said Stevie. "But it sounded to me like Graber was innocent and this was all a lie—did it sound like that to you?"

"Yes, I guess so."

"So we know who—well, mostly—and what and where and when . . . but not why or how."

"And no one will believe us without the why and how," said Susan Carol.

Stevie remembered something Dick Jerardi had told him when he had asked him about how to get a good story. If it's important, Jerardi had said, you have to get someone on the record. Otherwise, it's too easy for people to shoot you down.

"We have to do two things," he said. "We have to find out what exactly is going on here. And we have to get someone to go on the record."

"Well," Susan Carol said, snapping the notebook shut, "it's a sure bet that Professor Whiting isn't going to fill us in."

"Which leaves one person," Stevie said.

"Right. Chip Graber."

"Yup. We have to figure out a way to get him to tell the story on the record. And if we get him to say he's being blackmailed, then—"

"Hold on, hold on," she said. "How are we even going to

talk to Chip Graber? Even if we knew where MSU was staying, there'll be security all over the hotel. We'll never get close to him."

She was right, of course. Maybe they could wait until after the games tomorrow and try to talk to him in the locker room. No, that would be impossible; the locker rooms would be overrun with people. Maybe he could somehow hitch a ride on the golf cart with Roger Valdiserri and talk to him then. That wasn't likely, either. They had to get to him before the games tomorrow and they had to somehow get to him alone.

"First we have to find out where they're staying," he said. "My guess is that won't be too hard. The hard part will be getting into the hotel and finding him."

"No kidding," she said.

"What's the old saying?" he said. "Where there's a will, there's a way? We have the will. We'll figure out the way."

■ ■ ■

Finding out where Minnesota State was staying wasn't that hard at all. They remembered that there was a media workroom in their hotel basement, and in it, Susan Carol spotted a book labeled *Media Final Four Information* sitting among the team media guides and press releases promoting products and press conferences. One was headlined "Papa John's Pizza invites you to meet Dick Vitale!" Another was for a book signing for Dale Brown, the ex-LSU coach who was still a big name in New Orleans.

Stevie picked up the information book and began paging through it. Sure enough, there was a section on hotels. And in the hotel section there was a listing of the team hotels. "Atlanta Regional Champion—Downtown Marriott," it said. Minnesota State had advanced to the Final Four by winning the regional in Atlanta.

"Bingo!" he said, pointing at the listing.

"Bingo—maybe," Susan Carol said. "I remember Coach K telling me that when Duke is in the Final Four, they never stay in their assigned hotel because they want to get the team away from all the crazy stuff going on downtown. See, it says there that the Syracuse Regional Champion is staying at the Embassy Suites. Mr. Brill told me Duke is really staying in a Radisson by the airport. MSU may not be at the Marriott."

"Or they might be. Coach Graber isn't as experienced at going to the Final Four as Coach K. Let's find out."

He walked over to a bank of phones labeled COURTESY PHONES—LOCAL CALLS AND CREDIT CARD CALLS ONLY. As instructed on the phone, he dialed 9, and then, looking at the Marriott phone number in the information book, he dialed the hotel. Susan Carol started to ask him what he was doing, but he put a hand up when the phone was answered on the first ring.

"Hi, I'm trying to reach Professor Thomas Whiting?" he said. Susan Carol looked horrified. "He's with the Minnesota State basketball team."

He smiled when he heard the operator's answer. "Oh, really? No, that's okay, thanks." He hung up.

"What happened?" Susan Carol said.

"She said that all phone calls to people with the

Minnesota State team were being blocked and I could leave a message if I wanted."

"Which, of course, you didn't."

"No way! Okay, that's the easy part. Now, how do we get into the hotel and find Chip Graber? If they're blocking calls to people's rooms, they certainly aren't letting people roam around the hotel."

Susan Carol looked at her watch. "My father's expecting me upstairs any minute. We're supposed to go to dinner with a friend of his who lives here in town. There's no way I can get out of it."

Stevie and his dad had been invited to dinner by a group of the coaches from Philadelphia at some hot shot New Orleans restaurant called K-Paul's. When his dad had told him about the dinner, he had been excited at the prospect of eating with Fran Dunphy, the Penn coach he'd interviewed at the Palestra, and Jay Wright, the coach at Villanova. Now all he could think about was the entire evening being wasted. There wasn't much they could do.

"I think we need to get an early start in the morning," he said. "The first game isn't until five o'clock. That means the coaches won't want the players up too early, so we can probably catch him in his room."

"Why don't we leave here at eight-thirty," she said. "It can't be too far away if it's in downtown."

"The question is, what do we tell our dads?"

She looked baffled for a second, then snapped her fingers. "Easy. Remember when Mr. Brill was saying there's an entire room filled with radio stations doing broadcasts over at the coaches' hotel?"

"Yeah, so?"

"So we'll tell them we were invited over there by a couple of radio stations to appear, and Mr. Brill and Mr. Weiss said we should do it because it would be good publicity for the USBWA."

"And what if they say they want to go with us?"

"Chances are my dad won't want to. He said something about wanting to go to a museum in the morning. And if they do, let's just tell them we'd sort of like to do this on our own."

Stevie thought his dad would probably buy that, since they always argued over how much independence Stevie should be allowed at home. "Good idea," he said. "I think that can work."

They got on the elevator to head to their rooms. Stevie's floor came first. As he got off, he turned back to Susan Carol. "I'll see you at eight-thirty in that lower lobby, okay?" he said.

She gave him a nervous smile that reminded him how very pretty she was. "I hope you sleep tonight," she said. "I know I won't."

The door closed. She was right again. He knew he wouldn't sleep at all. There was just much too much to think about. And worry about.

8: A NEW FRIEND

STEVIE WOULD HAVE LAUGHED if someone had told him he would spend an evening in the presence of four college basketball coaches—Fran Dunphy had brought Harvard coach Frank Sullivan and Billy Hahn, the ex-La Salle coach, with him—wondering when it would be time to go home and go to bed. But that's pretty much what happened. The coaches took turns telling stories that normally Stevie would have been fascinated to hear. Sullivan, who seemed very un-coachlike to Stevie, with his soft-spoken manner and easy smile, talked about how close Harvard had come to landing Wally Szczerbiak a few years earlier.

"You mean *the* Wally Szczerbiak?" Stevie's dad asked as Sullivan told the story.

"The one who is an All-Star in Minnesota right now,"

Sullivan said. "We had him until the last minute. Then Miami of Ohio came in and, well, they were in a better basketball league than the Ivy League—"

"Wait a minute," Bill Thomas said, breaking in. "You're telling me a kid turned down Harvard to go to Miami of Ohio because the Mid-American Conference is a better basketball league than the Ivy League?"

Sullivan laughed. "Are you kidding? When you recruit a basketball player, he thinks of himself as a basketball player first and foremost. The student part comes second."

"Unless he's not a very good player," Dunphy put in.

"But Penn has had some very good teams," Stevie said to Dunphy.

"That's because kids think of us as a basketball school," Dunphy said. "Same with Princeton. But Frank and the other coaches in the league fight the notion that basketball isn't a serious sport at their schools."

"But turning down Harvard?" Stevie's dad said again.

"Happens all the time," Sullivan said. "Every once in a while we get lucky and there's a kid who is a good player and a good student who has been overlooked by the big-time schools. That's what happened with Szczerbiak . . . until the very end. Once Miami got involved, we were done."

Later, Hahn regaled them with stories about Maryland coach Gary Williams, who had a reputation for being perhaps the most intense coach in the profession. Hahn had worked for Williams for twelve years. "One night we're playing North Carolina," Hahn said. "We're down thirteen at halftime. Gary is ballistic. We're in his office right off the locker room and he looks at Dave Dickerson, one of our assistants, and he says, 'Look at you, you're not even sweating! You don't even care that we're losing! How can you *not* be sweating?' From that day forward, Dave always wore a heavy vest under his suit jacket to make sure he sweated."

Everyone laughed, and Hahn went on. Stevie should have been in heaven hearing these inside stories, but he couldn't stop looking at his watch. He wondered where Chip Graber was at that moment. He wondered what Susan Carol was doing. The only good news about the evening was that he and his dad got back to the hotel so late that he fell into bed and was so exhausted he went right to sleep.

He was up by six and lay awake in bed staring at the clock. He had told his dad in the cab coming back from the restaurant about how he and Susan Carol were planning to go to the coaches' hotel in the morning to do a couple of radio interviews. His dad was so proud and excited that Stevie had started to feel bad about lying. Then his dad gave him a sideways look and said, "So, you and Susan Carol are hitting it off okay then, huh?"

"Yeah, okay," Stevie said. "I mean, she's all right. At least she seems to know about basketball."

"Quite a concession coming from the world's leading expert on the subject," his dad said.

"Cut it out, Dad, I'm not an expert. I just like it."

"But you concede Susan Carol may know something about it, too."

"Actually, she knows quite a lot."

Even in the darkness of the cab, Stevie could see his dad

smile. "Wow. A girl who knows a lot about basketball. *And* she's pretty."

"Daaaad . . ."

"Okay, okay."

Stevie felt himself blush slightly just remembering the conversation. Maybe, he thought, in a year I'll be taller than . . . He pushed the thought from his mind. He was still trying to formulate a plan to find Chip once he and Susan Carol got to the hotel.

He took a shower, then waited impatiently until seven o'clock, when he woke his dad to tell him he wanted to go down to breakfast by seven-thirty. The first people they saw when they walked into the terrace restaurant were the Andersons.

"Looks like we're raising a couple of media stars, eh, Bill?" Reverend Anderson said, waving the Thomases over to the table.

"Yeah, how about that?" Stevie's dad said as they walked over. The two men shook hands and Stevie made a point of acting casual when he said good morning to Susan Carol. He noticed that she did the same thing, barely managing a hello as Stevie and his dad sat down to join them. She was dressed a lot more casually than the day before, wearing a gray sweatshirt that said GOLDSBORO BASKETBALL and jeans. Stevie had also put on jeans, causing his dad to ask if he shouldn't dress a bit more neatly to make his debut as a media star.

"Dad, it's *radio*," he said.

"Yes, I know," his father said. "But it would be nice to

make a good impression on the people interviewing you, wouldn't it?"

If his mother had been there, a full-scale argument would no doubt have ensued. His father didn't bother. Stevie was actually relieved to see that Susan Carol's thinking was the same as his: the more casual and unthreatening they looked, the better.

"I see your media star likes blue jeans as much as mine does," Reverend Anderson said.

Stevie and Susan Carol couldn't help smiling at one another. Clearly, the same fashion conversation had taken place in the Andersons' room that morning.

Breakfast consisted mostly of the fathers comparing notes on dinner the night before and where each was going to be sitting that night. Reverend Anderson said that a member of his church was a Duke season-ticket holder and had gotten him a seat in the Duke section. "Probably a better location than what I dug up," Bill Thomas said. "But at least I'm in the building."

By eight-fifteen, Stevie was ready to bolt. Susan Carol, clearly able to read his mind, said, "Dad, I think Stevie and I ought to get going."

"I thought you said your first interview was at nine," Reverend Anderson said.

"It is, but we should probably get there a little early just to be sure."

If either father was the least bit suspicious, they didn't show it. There really wasn't anything for them to be suspicious about. The radio story was a good one. Stevie's dad had been in the Hilton before and had seen "radio row," so he knew they weren't making it up.

Stevie and Susan Carol stood up to go.

"Wait—how are you getting there? When will you be back?" Stevie's dad asked.

Good questions. There was no way to know how long they would need to accomplish—or not accomplish—their mission.

As always, Susan Carol had it covered. "There's a shuttle service from here to the Hilton. We'll be fine. And how about we all meet back here around lunchtime. Like noon?"

"Okay," Reverend Anderson said. "But remember, I have to be at the church at two o'clock."

"Got it." She gave her father a kiss. "I'll call if we're held up." They headed for the escalator that would take them to the lobby.

"Church on Saturday?" Stevie asked as they made their way down.

"Yup. He started a Saturday Bible study group about two years ago for people who were addicted to sports, and it's sort of taken off around the country. He's visiting the New Orleans group while he's here."

He looked at her to see if she was joking. She didn't appear to be.

They were walking through the lobby with Susan Carol clearly leading the way. "Do you know where we're going?" he said, deciding a change of subject was safest.

"Yes," she said. "I asked for directions when we got back last night. The Marriott's on Canal and Chartres. It's kind of a long walk from here, but there really is a shuttle to the Hilton that puts us only about four blocks away."

That was fine with Stevie. As eager as he was to get the morning started, he was already dreading their arrival at the hotel. How were they going to find Chip Graber? What if they got arrested? That would give Reverend Anderson something to talk about at Bible study.

Once they were on the shuttle bus, Stevie asked if Susan Carol had a plan.

"It's hard to know until we get there. There probably won't be any way to get onto the floors where the team is staying—unless you have some kind of proof you're with the team."

"Okay, how do we get that?" he asked.

"Beats me," she said. "That's why I think we have to check the place out and then come up with a plan."

Stevie would have much preferred having a plan going in, but he had nothing. It wasn't like they could use a house phone in the lobby, call up to his room, and say, "Chip, we're here, what room are you in?" They were too young to be delivery people. Too young to be room service or house-keeping. And darn, he'd left his suction cups at home, so they couldn't scale the building. . . . Susan Carol was right. They would have to find out what they were up against, then decide what to do.

They got off the shuttle at the Hilton and started to walk. The streets weren't as choked with people as they had been the night before, when Stevie and his dad had taken the taxi back to the hotel, but they were crowded. Every street corner had vendors selling "official NCAA merchandise." Stevie remembered reading an item in the paper about how part of the NCAA's deal with the city of New Orleans included a promise from the police to arrest anyone selling nonofficial merchandise. Stevie glanced at the prices as they walked by one official vendor and noticed that the T-shirts were going for twenty-five dollars. No wonder the NCAA wanted to make everyone buy their stuff.

Stevie could feel his heart starting to pound a little bit as they approached the hotel. There were people milling around everywhere and Stevie noticed a couple of large men in sunglasses with little wires coming out of their ears. Security people. "Just keep walking as if we belong inside the hotel," Susan Carol said quietly as they approached the entrance. Stevie tried not to look too closely at the security men. They weren't stopping people, though, just kind of standing around looking the crowd over. Stevie and Susan Carol walked in without anyone saying anything. Stevie breathed a sigh of relief. At least they were inside.

The lobby was a madhouse. Almost everyone seemed to be wearing purple and white. Clearly, this wasn't just the MSU team hotel but also the hotel where all their fans were staying.

"This is why Coach K told me Duke doesn't stay in the assigned hotel," Susan Carol said, sweeping a hand around the lobby. "He doesn't want his players having to walk through all their fans every time they leave their room."

Stevie could see where that might be a problem. "Bad for

us, I think," he said. "Means the players are even less likely to show up in the lobby."

"Maybe. Or we could make it work for us," she said. "Let's see what this place looks like."

Before Stevie could ask her what she meant, she was working her way around the lobby. The front desk was to the right of the door, but there was no point in going there. They could see an elevator bank a few steps beyond the front desk. "Just keep walking until somebody stops us," Susan Carol said.

The stopping point was at the elevator bank. There were two more security guards there and a large sign that said HOTEL GUESTS ONLY. PLEASE HAVE KEY READY FOR INSPECTION.

Susan Carol didn't hesitate as they approached the checkpoint. "Morning," she said, sounding cool as could be, waving a hand at the guards as if she'd walked past them a dozen times already.

"Miss, I need to see your key," one of the guards said, taking a quick step to get between Susan Carol and the elevators.

Susan Carol put a hand up to her mouth as if she had done something awful. "Oh my goodness," she said, her voice suddenly Southern. Stevie thought he counted about six syllables in the word "goodness." "Steve, did you remember to bring a key? I just plain forgot maahn."

Stevie stumbled for a second before picking up his cue. "I thought *you* had it," he said.

Susan Carol looked imploringly at the guard, eyes opening wide. "Sir, I am *so* sorry. My brother and I *both* forgot our keys. I can't believe we were so stupid. I promise it will never happen again."

For a minute Stevie thought the wide-eyed-Southern-girl charm was going to work. But the guard said, "I really am sorry, but we just can't let anyone up without their key. If you just go to the front desk, tell the people there what room you're in, and show them some ID . . ."

"I don't have any ID!" Susan Carol practically shrieked. Stevie thought she was going to cry.

"Well, you can call up to your room and have someone come down. . . ."

"Our dad's not in the room. He went out for a run, a long run. We don't know when he'll be back."

"Well then, if you ask for the manager and tell him the problem, maybe he can help." He smiled again. "Because even if I let you by, miss, if there's no one in the room, and you haven't got a key, how are you going to get in?"

Great, Stevie thought. They had found the one security man on earth with common sense. Susan Carol actually had tears in her eyes.

"I really *am* sorry," the security man said. "I'm sure the manager can help you, or you can wait here in the lobby until your dad comes back."

Susan Carol looked at Stevie as if he might have an idea. He had nothing. "Okay," Susan Carol sighed. "Thank you."

"You're very welcome. Good luck."

They walked away. "Good try," Stevie said.

"Thought I had him there for a minute," she said, any sign of near hysteria long gone.

"Well, don't feel too bad," he said. "If we had gotten through, that still wouldn't have put us on the right floor."

"I'd guess they're on the top floor or close to it," she said.

That made sense. He wished he had thought of it.

"Come on, let's see what else we can find down here," she said. "I never thought it would be that easy anyway."

They began a tour of the lobby. There was a large bar opposite the front desk, with people sitting everywhere, looking up at various TV sets that were tuned to ESPN. Vitale, Fowler, and Phelps were now on some sort of set and, not surprisingly, Vitale was talking. Stevie couldn't hear what he was saying, but he was waving his arms while Phelps and Fowler watched with bemused looks on their faces. Next to the lobby bar was another official NCAA merchandise stand. This time Stevie noticed the price of the caps—twenty-two bucks.

They kept walking. On the left side of the lobby in the back was another entrance from a side street. Stevie could see cars pulling up to the door when the glass doors opened as they walked by. There was also a restaurant back there and a line of people waiting to get in for breakfast.

"Any ideas?" he said.

"Not so far," she said. Then she pointed across the lobby.

"There's an escalator over there. Let's see if we can get up one floor. Maybe there are meeting rooms up there or something. We might get lucky."

Given the luck they were having so far, Stevie didn't see any reason not to try the escalator. They picked their way through still more people, past a Starbucks coffee stand where there was also a line, and up the escalator. It was relatively quiet on the mezzanine level. Susan Carol had been right: there were meeting rooms, but they all appeared empty. They checked some of the signs to see if, by some chance, one said "Minnesota State Purple Tide." Nothing.

"We're getting nowhere fast," he said.

"Don't give up yet," she said.

They walked past another elevator bank, which, of course, had security people and the same sign about needing a key. "We could try those guys," he said. "Your act might work on them."

She shook her head. "Last resort. We don't want word getting out around the hotel that two kids are trying to crash. Then we have no chance."

They rounded a corner and saw a large banner on the wall that said KFPT—ANCHOR STATION FOR THE MINNESOTA STATE PURPLE TIDE RADIO NETWORK. There was a table set up in front of the banner with microphones and some radio equipment. There was a man seated behind the table fiddling with the equipment. With no place else to go at the moment, Susan Carol and Stevie walked over to the radio setup.

Stevie had no idea what they were going to say to the man or even why they would say anything to him, except that he appeared to have at least a distant connection to MSU. Susan Carol, naturally, knew just what to say.

"Are you one of the Minnesota State broadcasters?" she said, sounding slightly breathless again.

The man looked up at her and smiled. "No, honey," he said. "I'm just the engineer for the network."

Susan Carol didn't miss a beat. "Wow," she said. "An engineer. That must be cool. Are you guys broadcasting from here today?"

The man looked at his watch. "In just about an hour," he said. "If I can get this equipment to work."

"Do you ever get to meet the players?" Susan Carol asked.

Again, the man smiled benevolently at the pretty girl asking questions. "I know all of them," he said. "We travel with the team and interview the players and coaches before and after games."

Susan Carol now looked as if she had just met either the president or the Pope. "Goodness. Will any of them be on this morning?"

He laughed. "No, not this morning. Kind of a big game tonight, you know. We'll have one of the assistants on at some point, we don't know when. And we have a couple of reporters coming over. But no players today." He looked at Susan Carol, who now looked very, very sad. "Bet you'd like to meet Chip Graber, huh?"

"It would be the happiest moment of my life," Susan Carol said. Stevie noticed that she had abandoned the thick Southern accent. "I am a *huge* Purple Tide fan. My name is Susan Carol. Susan Carol Anderson." She put out her hand.

He took it and said, "Susan Carol, nice to meet you. I'm Jerry Ventura—no, no relation to the former governor."

Ventura then shook hands with Stevie. "And you are?"

"Stevie." There, that was his brilliant entry into the conversation.

"So, where are you kids from?" Ventura asked.

"We live in Duluth now," Susan Carol said. "But we've only lived there a couple years. We lived in North Carolina until then."

"I thought I heard a little bit of an accent in your voice," Ventura said.

"Stevie here is still kind of a Duke fan, but I'm for MSU all the way."

"I am *not*," Stevie protested.

Susan Carol just smiled. "So, Mr. Ventura, what do you think—will it be Duke and MSU in the final?"

"Yeah, that's where my money'd be."

They chatted about the team's chances while Stevie marveled at Susan Carol's gift of gab. She had, for lack of a better word, an *adultness* about her that he knew he couldn't touch. As if to prove his point, Jerry Ventura drew him into the conversation by saying, "So, Stevie, how much younger are you than your sister?"

Stevie knew this was his moment to play along. "Three years," he said without hesitating. "I'm in the eighth grade."

If the idea that Susan Carol was an eleventh grader threw Jerry at all, he didn't show it.

"So, Mr. Ventura, what hotel do all you radio people stay in?" she said, without giving him a chance to respond to Stevie's claim of a three-year age difference.

"Oh, we're here," he said. "And call me Jerry. I'm not that old, you know."

Stevie began to get an idea of where Susan Carol was going with this. Her smile was now so bright he thought he might need sunglasses. "You *really* get to stay here with all the players?" she said. "That must be so cool! You're right on the same floor with them and everything?"

"No, not the same floor," he said. "They've got all the players and coaches way up on the top floors—forty and forty-one. But we're on the concierge floor, the sixteenth. The rooms are really nice."

"Oh, I've heard about that," Susan Carol said. "Don't they have a really nice lounge where you can get drinks and things?"

"Oh yeah," Jerry said importantly. "The breakfasts are great."

"Speaking of which, I'm thirsty. Stevie, maybe we should go back down to the restaurant and try again. There was the longest line before—you wouldn't believe . . ."

Jerry smiled at Susan Carol. "Look, if you kids just want a drink, you can go on up to the concierge lounge and get something there."

"Could we?" Susan Carol said, her tone implying that the offer was roughly the equivalent of being given the keys to Fort Knox.

Jerry reached into his pocket and pulled out a key. "Here, take my key. You'll need it to get to the floor. There's a slot in the elevator, you just put the key into it and then press 16."

Stevie was now officially amazed by Susan Carol. Okay, he thought, let's take the key and run. But she wasn't finished yet.

As Jerry was handing her the key, she said, "Just in

case someone asks us for a room number when we get up there . . ."

"Good thought," Jerry said. "They do ask in there sometimes. It's 1607."

"Thanks. We'll be back in a flash."

"Take your time," he said. "We don't go on for another forty-five minutes."

Stevie could not believe Susan Carol had pulled this off. They could now wave Jerry's key at the security guards and go directly to the top floor. Of course, they still had to figure out what room on the top floor belonged to Chip Graber.

They waved goodbye to their new best friend and headed for the elevator bank. Susan Carol held up the key as they walked by the security people and said, "He's with me," just in case they decided to question Stevie. The key had magic powers. They nodded and moved aside.

"Now what—" he started to say as she punched the elevator button.

"Shhh. I'll tell you in a minute."

The elevator arrived, filled with people in purple and white. They got on and Susan Carol took Jerry's key, put it in the slot, and pressed 16.

"But he said—"

"Shhh," she said again. He was starting to feel as if he *was* her little brother.

There were four stops before they reached 16. Stevie felt as if each stop was taking about ten minutes. Finally, they reached 16 and Susan Carol practically pushed Stevie off the elevator.

"Where are we going?" he demanded once they were alone in the hallway.

"First, we're going to that lounge to get sodas, so we have something to show Jerry when we go back downstairs. Second, we're going to his room."

"His room, why?"

"My dad was a chaplain for the Carolina Panthers for a few years."

"The football team?"

"Yes. A couple times a year, he would go on road trips with them. He took me once and I remember that there was a rooming list because the phones to the team's rooms were blocked the way the MSU phones are blocked here."

"And you think this guy will have a rooming list."

She held up the key and said, "There's only one way to find out."

9: FINDING CHIP GRABER

THEY DIDN'T LINGER in the concierge lounge very long. They nodded to the lady at the desk—who didn't ask them for a room number and seemed decidedly uninterested in their presence—grabbed two sodas, and headed for room 1607.

There was no one around, so Susan Carol slid the key card into the door. The green light came on and they pushed their way into the room.

"Anybody here?" Susan Carol asked.

There was no response and they walked into the room, which had two double beds in it, one of them made, the other unmade.

"I had a sudden fear that he might be rooming with someone," Susan Carol said.

"What would you have done if someone had answered?" he said.

She smiled. "I have no idea. Let's check this place out fast and get out of here. We need to go downstairs, get another key, and get this one back to Jerry."

"Another key?"

"We have to give this one back to him, right?" she said. "We don't know how long any of this is going to take, or if we're going to need to come back. We need a key of our own."

"You know, you're starting to worry me, Susan Carol. Lying, breaking and entering, searching people's rooms . . ."

"We're not really breaking . . . just entering. Now shut up and look."

They went to work. Susan Carol took the bedside table and Stevie put his soda down on the corner of the desk and began going through a pile of papers. There were statistics sheets and media guides for Minnesota State and St. Joe's. There was a notebook and a room service menu. Beneath the room service menu was a stack of papers, including one that said "MSU Itinerary for Final Four Weekend" on it. Stevie looked through it quickly and noticed that the Purple Tide was scheduled to fly home Tuesday morning and arrive in time for a "national championship victory celebration—12 noon—Heavenly Coffee Field House." He remembered reading a story about many MSU alumni being upset that the name of C. W. Whitaker, the first president of the school, had been taken off the field house when the coffee company offered $3 million a year to get its name on the building.

He snorted at the planned victory celebration and was starting to move on to the next piece of paper on the pile when there was a knock on the door. Stevie froze. It couldn't be Jerry, could it? Susan Carol put a finger to her lips to indicate that he shouldn't say anything. There was another knock. "Go away, go away," Stevie hissed under his breath.

They heard a key go into the slot. Stevie felt himself panicking. What should they do? Hide? Where? He made a dive for behind the bed, knocking a sheaf of paper onto the floor. Then he heard a voice from outside say, "Housekeeping."

Susan Carol bolted toward the door. "Sorry," she said as a maid poked her head inside the room. "We didn't hear you knock, I guess. We'll be out of here in just a few minutes."

Stevie couldn't really see the maid's face, but he heard her say, "Oh, okay. Sorry. I'll come back."

She pulled the door shut and Susan Carol bolted it. Stevie sat down on the bed. He was pouring sweat all of a sudden.

"That was terrifying," he said.

She sat down next to him. He noticed her face was drained of color. "I know," she said. She put her hand on his hand, which made him feel good but also made him sweat even more. "Let's find this thing and get out of here."

They started to pick up the papers he'd knocked to the floor, and there it was: "Rooming List, Minnesota State Purple Tide, April 1–5."

"Got it!" he said. He put a finger at the top and worked

his way down to the G's. "Here it is," he said, "Graber, Alan Jr.—room 4101."

"All the way at the top," she said. "Figures. See who he's rooming with."

Stevie continued down the page. There wasn't another 4101. He went through the list again to be sure. As he did, something caught his eye. Tom Richards, another of the seniors, was in 4103, and he couldn't find anyone else in there. He checked on the other two seniors—Marlin Bennett and Tammu Abate—and saw they had single rooms, too.

"All the seniors are in singles," he said. "And they're all at that end of the hall."

She nodded. "Okay, let's get out of here before the maid comes back."

Stevie quickly tried to rearrange the desk to approximate the way he had found it. He wasn't sure where the rooming list had been, but it had been near the bottom of the pile, so he put it back there.

"Don't forget your soda," Susan Carol said. Then, poking their heads out the door to make sure no one was around, they headed back down the hallway.

"What now?" he asked.

"First we get a duplicate key. Then we give this one back to Jerry and *then* we go try to find Chip."

"We'll have to tell Jerry why we aren't going to hang around to hear the show."

"I know," she said. "I'll think of an excuse before we get there."

They took the elevator back down to the first floor, making several interminable stops for MSU fans. Stevie was beginning to think the people in purple and white were like those furry little animals on *Star Trek* called Tribbles, which reproduced every few minutes until the *Enterprise* was overrun with them. They were everywhere.

They finally made it back to the lobby. Amazingly, the area around the front desk was quiet. Susan Carol chose a middle-aged man with a small black mustache as her next victim.

"May I help you, young lady?" he said as the two of them walked up.

"Oh yes, I hope so," she said. "We're in room 1607 and our key isn't working."

"Oh, I'm so sorry," he said. She had been holding the key out, and he took it and slid it across the counter and into some kind of garbage can beneath the desk. Seeing the key disappear unnerved Stevie. What if he didn't give them a new one?

"Last name?" he asked

"Ventura," she said. "My dad's name is Jerry." She leaned forward and spoke in a whisper as if she didn't want anyone to hear what she was about to tell the man, whose name tag said he was Vincent DeFriest—Brooklyn, N.Y. "We're with the Minnesota State team. I think we're listed separately from the other guests."

"You are," Mr. DeFriest said. "Here you are."

He went over to a key machine, punched some buttons, and produced a new key card. He handed it to

Susan Carol, and Stevie felt his heart start up again.

"Anything else I can help you with, Miss Ventura?" he asked.

"Won't I need a new card for my dad?" she asked.

"Oh yes, of course you will. New code and all. I'm sorry." He punched buttons on the machine again and produced a second key.

"Thank you so much," she said with her best Southern manners.

Stevie thought he saw Mr. DeFriest turn just a tad pink. "You are very welcome," he said.

They headed back to the escalator. Stevie had come up with an excuse for Jerry. "Let's tell Jerry we just saw our dad and he wants us to go with him to Bible study class," he said.

She gave him a look to see if he was being sarcastic.

He wasn't. "He can't question something like that," he said.

"You're right," she said.

The two hosts were at the table, wearing headsets, when they got back to the KFPT broadcast position. Susan Carol handed Jerry the key, held up her soda, and said, "Thanks, Jerry, you saved us from a long wait in line."

Jerry gave her a big smile, then swept his hand in the direction of the two hosts, tapping one on the shoulder to get his attention. The guy glanced up with an annoyed look on his face. When he saw Susan Carol standing in front of him, the look was replaced by a smile and he pulled off his headset.

"Mike, this is the girl, um, I mean, these are the kids I was telling you about," Jerry said.

Mike put out a hand to Susan Carol. "Mike Lombardo, voice of the Purple Tide, young lady, nice to meet you." He turned to his partner, who had also pulled off his headset. "This is my color commentator, Trey Woods."

Stevie recognized the name. Trey Woods had played for Minnesota State in the eighties. The reason he knew that was because Chip Graber had broken his all-time scoring record at the school earlier in the season. Woods also shook hands with Susan Carol. She turned to Stevie, who was beginning to feel invisible, and said, "This is my brother, Steve."

"Nice to meet you, kid," Mike Lombardo said as Stevie came close enough so they could shake hands. Trey Woods also offered his hand—which was huge—but couldn't seem to find anything to say to him.

"So, Jerry tells me you kids are big Purple Tide fans," Lombardo said.

"Absolutely," Susan Carol said. "We can't wait for tonight."

She was doing the big-smile bit again.

"Well, that's great. Jerry said you wanted to hang around and watch us do the show. We're on in about ten minutes and . . ."

Susan Carol was now shaking her head as if a truly awful thing had just happened. "We really would *love* to watch you do the show, but our dad just reminded us that we promised to go to Bible study with him."

"Bible study?" Trey Woods said. "Good for you. Praise the Lord in all ways at all times."

Mike Lombardo didn't seem nearly as thrilled about their plans for the morning. "You kids big God-squadders or something?" he asked.

Stevie noticed Trey Woods visibly flinch.

"I guess you could say that," Susan Carol said. "My dad is a minister."

"Oh, I see," Lombardo said, clearly a little embarrassed.

"A minister," Trey Woods said. "I'm a minister, too."

Now it was Lombardo's turn to flinch.

"Really?" said Susan Carol.

"Oh yes," Woods said. "I was ordained online last year. I'm a minister of the Church of Righteous-Thinking Athletes." He leaned toward Susan Carol. "Someday you and I will pray together." He didn't make the same offer to Stevie. Hallelujah for that, Stevie thought.

"Praise the Lord," Susan Carol answered, her smile beginning to waver.

"Five minutes to air," Jerry Ventura said—four of the sweetest words Stevie had ever heard.

Susan Carol pumped Jerry's hand. "Thanks again, Jerry. It was great to meet all you guys. *Please* be sure to bring home a Purple Tide victory tonight, okay?"

"We'll do the best we can," Lombardo said.

"Praise the Lord," Trey Woods said, clasping both of Susan Carol's hands in his massive paws. "I hope we meet again, young lady."

"Oh gee, me too," Susan Carol said, appearing just a bit unnerved.

Stevie was now firmly convinced the guy was an out-

and-out weirdo and decided he would have thought that even if he hadn't been ordained online. He waved half-heartedly and turned away, hoping Susan Carol would follow. She appeared to be having a little bit of trouble extricating herself from Trey Woods's grip. "Come *on*, Susan Carol. Dad's waiting," he said.

"Thanks," she said after they were away. "He was creepy."

Their new key whisked them by security one more time. Once on the elevator, Susan Carol pressed the button for the forty-first floor. Stevie felt his heart starting to race again.

"You ready?" he said to Susan Carol as the elevator shot upward.

"Ready," she said. "But we aren't there yet. There could be security on the floor."

"Or he might not be there right now," Stevie said.

"That's not a problem," she said, holding up the magic key. "We can come back."

They were alone on the elevator all the way up, a pleasant surprise. There was no sign of security when the elevator doors opened on 41, which was an even more pleasant surprise.

"So far, so good," Susan Carol said.

They got off the elevator and glanced around—no one in sight. They followed the sign pointing to rooms 4101 through 4115. Two-thirds of the way down, the hallway veered to the right. Stevie was thinking about what their opening line would be when they got to Graber's door, when he heard a voice say, "Hold on there, kids, where do you think you're going?"

He looked up and saw a security guard, who had been sitting in a chair just around the corner. He stood up to a height that Stevie estimated to be at least six foot eight and blocked them from going any farther. Peering around him, Stevie could see the door to 4101. They were *so* close. . . . But, looking at the giant in their path, still *so* far.

As usual, Susan Carol was cool as could be.

"Oh, hey," she said. "We're just going to see Chip."

The guard narrowed his eyes, looked down at Susan Carol without even the hint of a smile, and said, "There's no visitors allowed up here. Players and coaches only on this end of the floor. You should have been stopped getting off the elevator. I don't know where my partner is." He reached for a walkie-talkie in his pocket.

"Hang on there, buddy, don't get all bent out of shape," Stevie said, suddenly emboldened for reasons he could not have explained if asked. "Chip's my cousin, he's in room 4101, and he's expecting to see me before the team leaves for the game. He'll be pretty pissed off if he finds out you wouldn't let us get in to see him."

He felt very adult saying "pissed off." The guard gave him a look, too, but it was different from the one he had given Susan Carol. There was just a hint of doubt in his eyes. Or maybe it was just the angle, since his eyes were so much higher up than Stevie's. "And who is she?" he said, pointing at Susan Carol.

Before Stevie could stammer out an answer, Susan Carol said, "I'm his girlfriend."

The giant looked at Susan Carol, then looked at Stevie. "You like 'em short, huh, kid?" he said to her.

Stevie started to say something, but Susan Carol gave him a look that made him think twice. "Okay, you say Chip's expecting you," the guard said. "Well, he didn't say anything to me about it and the coaches said no guests— especially girls."

Stevie's heart sank. They were going to be turned away five yards from Chip Graber's door.

"Tell you what, though," the giant went on, "we'll go knock on Chip's door. You know his room number, so I guess it's possible you're telling the truth. We'll just go find out. But I'll tell you this much: *if* you're lying, I'm calling the cops and you're going to be arrested for trespassing."

Stevie didn't think they could be arrested for trespassing in a hotel, but since they weren't guests, maybe they could be. At the very least, they were going to be in a heap of trouble. He wondered if perhaps they should run while they still had a chance to escape. He was mulling all this over when he heard Susan Carol say, "And when Chip confirms our story, I'm sure you'll apologize to us, won't you?"

What was she doing? Why in the world would Chip confirm their story?

The giant and Susan Carol were both walking toward the door. There was no escape now. He squared his shoulders and caught up to them just as the giant was ringing the doorbell. Stevie couldn't ever remember seeing a hotel room that had a doorbell—not that he had seen that many. For a moment there was no answer. The giant had seemed pretty certain that Graber was in the room, but maybe he was wrong. Then Stevie heard footsteps coming in the direction of the door. He was suddenly aware that he was drenched in sweat. He glanced at Susan Carol. If she was nervous or scared, it didn't show. The door opened and Chip Graber, dressed in a white T-shirt that said MINNESOTA STATE, BIG TEN CHAMPIONS, a pair of purple sweatpants, and socks, stood staring at the three of them with what seemed to Stevie to be a very annoyed look.

"What's up?" he said to the guard, glancing first at Susan Carol, then at Stevie.

"These kids claim they're expected," the giant said. He pointed at Stevie. "This your cousin?"

Graber started to open his mouth but before he could say anything, Stevie jumped in. "Sorry we're late, Chip. Professor Whiting was giving us trouble just like you said he would."

The bored, annoyed look on Graber's face disappeared. He looked at Stevie, his eyes now a question mark. "Whiting?" he said. "Whiting gave you trouble?"

"Sure did," Stevie said. "Just like *yesterday*. Well, you know what a pain he can be. . . ."

Graber was clearly confused. A couple of seconds passed before he said anything. Each second felt like an hour to Stevie.

"Mike, I'm sorry," Graber finally said. "I shoulda told you my cousin was coming up. My bad, man."

Mike the Giant's face softened a little bit. "Chip, I thought you guys weren't supposed to have anybody . . ."

"Yeah, I know, Mike, but come on, it's my cousin. I haven't seen him since Christmas. It's all right, he's a good kid." He playfully pushed Stevie's shoulder. "He's a pain sometimes, but I told him he could come up for a few minutes."

Mike nodded. "Okay then. But don't let them stay too long. The schedule says you guys have a walk-through in the ballroom at noon."

"I know, Mike. Thanks."

Clearly baffled and disappointed, Mike turned to walk away. "No need to apologize," Stevie said. Before Mike could respond, Susan Carol shoved him hard from behind, pushing him into the room. Chip Graber had opened the door all the way, and Stevie almost fell on his face.

"What is it with boys?" she said. "You always have to have the last word."

"You were the one who brought up apologizing," he said, getting the last word.

Chip Graber closed the door and looked them up and down again. "Okay, you guys had better have a damn good explanation for what just happened."

They followed him into a large living room with a panoramic view of downtown New Orleans, all the way up to the Superdome and beyond. The TV was turned on and—surprise—there was Vitale, waving his arms. Stevie wondered if he ever slept.

Graber clicked off the TV, sat down on one of the

couches, and pointed to the two armchairs. Susan Carol sat in one, Stevie the other. Stevie was suddenly very thirsty and was shocked to notice he was still holding a can of soda. It had been a long, weird morning. . . .

"Okay, I'm going to give you guys about two minutes to tell me what the hell this is about and then I'm going to call Mike back in here and tell him you're frauds," he said. "So talk fast."

"The first thing you need to know is that we want to help you," Susan Carol said. "The second thing you need to know is we appreciate you backing us up out there. The third thing you need to know is if you do call Mike back in here, you'll have to explain to him why you said Stevie was your cousin."

If that thought bothered Graber at all, it didn't show.

"Yeah, yeah," he said. "Start by telling me who you are. Then tell me how the hell you got up here."

"My name is Stevie Thomas and this is Susan Carol Anderson."

"Keep going."

"We won't bore you with how we got up here," Susan Carol said, picking up the story. "We're in New Orleans because we won the U.S. Basketball Writers Association writing contest for kids."

"Reporters?" he said. "Kid reporters? Wait, you came up here to get a scoop? On the day of the game? You've gotta be freakin' kidding, right?"

Susan Carol leaned forward. "Chip, it was a complete accident, but we overheard your conversation with Professor

Whiting yesterday, and we want to try to help you."

"What conversation?" he said abruptly.

Stevie jumped in. "You had just arrived for practice. You and Whiting walked into the loading dock area to talk. We were there. We heard everything he said to you."

Chip Graber's face drained of all color. There was a long pause before he said anything. "Look, whatever you think you heard, you got it wrong," he said finally. "Professor Whiting, he and I, we were just joking around. That was all it was."

Susan Carol's voice was very soft now. "Chip, that didn't sound like a joke. It sounded like he was threatening you and your father. You need help. Heck, *we* need help. We couldn't hear that conversation and do nothing. So we came to you. . . ."

Chip stood up, and Stevie thought he was going to take them back to Mike. "Start at the beginning," he said. "How much do you know?"

10: CHIP'S STORY

SUSAN CAROL AND STEVIE walked Chip through their story. Graber listened to the whole thing without commenting, except when Susan Carol told him how she had talked her way past the guard at the arena so she could hear Whiting's voice in order to identify him.

"That was good thinking," he said.

"It was Steve's idea," she said quickly.

He then insisted that they explain how they had found him, and they went through that story, too. "Watch out for Mike Lombardo, he's kind of a letch," he said.

"The one who scared me was Trey Woods," Susan Carol said.

"He's harmless, I think," Graber said. "Nuts, but harmless." He leaned back on the couch. "You went through a lot to get up here."

He stared out the window for a minute. Stevie turned to see what he was staring at, but it was just the view. They waited. "Look," he finally continued, "I appreciate what you did and your concern. But there's really nothing you can do. There's probably nothing *I* can do, either."

"So you're just going to throw the championship game?" Susan Carol said.

"I didn't say that!" His eyes flashed angrily at the implication.

"Then let us help," Stevie said. "We're kids, but we're smart." He pointed at Susan Carol. "Especially her."

Graber smiled. "I don't doubt it. But I think we're overmatched here. To tell you the truth, I'm not even sure who we're up against."

"Tell us what you know," Susan Carol said. "We told you our story, now you tell us yours—you owe us that much."

He went back to staring out the window. Stevie was pretty sure he was trying to decide how much to trust them. He remembered something Dick Jerardi had said: "Sometimes the best question is the one you don't ask. Sometimes you just let the silence ask your question. Let it hang in the air until the other guy says something to fill up the space. They almost always do."

Finally, after what felt like forever, Graber stood up and walked over to the bar. He sat down on a bar stool, clasped his hands together, and leaned forward. "Okay, listen," he said. "If I tell you what I know, you have to promise that we are completely off the record, that you'll tell no one—including your fathers."

"We haven't told our fathers anything so far," Susan Carol said. "And we couldn't write anything now even if we wanted to. But you have our word. We won't say or write anything until and unless you tell us we can."

"Steve?" Graber said.

"What?" Stevie hesitated, remembering Jerardi's admonition to get people to talk on the record. But there was a lot more at stake here than a newspaper story. "Sure," he said finally. "Off the record is fine."

Chip got up, went around the bar, and took a Coke from the refrigerator. "You guys want one?" he asked. They both shook their heads.

"All right then," he said. "Here it is from the top.

"It started on Monday. We flew home from the regionals on Sunday night and we partied pretty late. First time in school history making the Final Four, it was a big deal. There must have been ten thousand people waiting for us at the gym when we pulled up."

"Heavenly Coffee Field House?" Stevie said.

Graber smiled. "Yeah, how sick is that? But we get free coffee all the time, so it's not so bad."

Susan Carol gave Stevie a look that clearly meant he should shut up and let Graber tell the story before he changed his mind. She was probably right.

"Anyway, I went to bed late, maybe around four, and I had no intention of getting up before noon."

"No classes?" Stevie said before he could stop himself,

causing Susan Carol to shoot him a look that said he was a complete moron.

"I only have Tuesday-Thursday classes. I knew I wasn't going to have enough credits to graduate on time anyway, so I took an underload this semester so I could concentrate on playing ball."

"Any of the other seniors going to graduate?"

This time it was Susan Carol talking, which surprised Stevie.

Graber smiled. "Put it this way: I'm closer than the other three guys."

"So you're the student-athlete in the group," Susan Carol said.

He laughed. "Yeah, that's me. We got a kick out of that guy in the press conference. Clearly, he hasn't been around too many basketball teams."

Stevie now thought he understood. Susan Carol had noticed that the questions were loosening him up.

"So I went to sleep. Turned off my cell. No one has the number at my house. . . ."

"You live with your parents?" Stevie said, surprised.

"No, no. I share a house with two other guys. Non–basketball players. It's about a mile from campus. Five-minute drive."

"You have a car?" Susan Carol said.

He laughed. "Every college basketball player has a car," he said. "Mine's a little different because my coach bought it for me, but it's legal—because he's my dad."

"So no one has your number," Stevie said, thinking

they needed to get the story moving a little faster.

"Right. I mean, my parents have it, my girlfriend has it, a few other people. Guys on the team. That's it. At nine a.m. the phone rings. I can't imagine who it is because just about everyone who has the number was up as late as I was. I pick it up and it's Professor Whiting. He says he needs to come over and see me right away, that something has come up.

"I say, 'Can't it wait until this afternoon?' He says it can't, that it is very important to my dad. I say, 'Okay then, give me half an hour to take a shower and get something to eat.' He says he'll bring bagels."

Stevie thought Graber was adding a lot of details they didn't need, but he knew they had to let him tell this his way. At least he was talking.

"So he comes over with bagels. I make coffee, we sit down. He says to me that there's a problem that, unfortunately, has to be dealt with and it is out of his hands and he's really, really sorry to be the one to have to tell me about this. I'm scared. I thought my dad was sick or something. But then I'm thinking if my dad was sick, why would Whiting be the one telling me? He's around the team a lot but he's not close to my dad or anything. I mean, he doesn't know anything about basketball. He's my ethics professor."

"Funny thing," Stevie said.

Graber looked at him quizzically for a second, then nodded his head. "Yeah, how about that," he said.

"So I ask him what the heck he's talking about and he finally says to me, 'Chip, there's a problem with your transcript.' I'm baffled. Look, I've never been much of a student. I've known all along that I want to play pro ball, and, unlike a lot of other guys, people tell me I'm not fooling myself."

"I remember reading that you would have been a lottery pick if you'd put your name in the draft last year," Susan Carol said.

He nodded. "Exactly. Probably one of the top ten picks. But I wanted to play one more year for my dad, and I knew we had a chance to be real good. Not many teams in the country have four senior starters. So I came back. I *did* have some academic problems last spring, but they all got resolved."

"What kind of problems?" Susan Carol asked.

He shook his head. "I flunked a class," he said.

"One class is a big deal?" Stevie was surprised.

"No, not by itself," he said. "But I've been on academic probation a couple of times. Silly stuff. Always happens in season because I get behind, especially in March when we're away from campus so much. At the end of my sophomore year, I was a couple classes shy of the NCAA minimums. I had to go to summer school so I could play my junior year—which I did. But that meant I was on probation. When I flunked that class in the spring, it put me back on probation."

"Which meant what?"

"It meant I couldn't flunk a class fall semester or I couldn't play."

"And did you?"

"No. But this is where it gets complicated. Whiting said that 'someone' had a transcript of mine that showed I flunked *two* classes last spring. I said that was impossible. That's when he *showed me* the transcript. Someone must have gone into the computer system at school and changed my grade in Econ 300 from a C+ to an F."

"Which would mean what?" Susan Carol asked.

"It would mean I wasn't eligible to play fall semester— our first twelve games of the season."

"Can't you just go to the Econ professor and get him to say something got messed up in the computer?"

"Professor Scott," Graber said. "Great guy."

"And?" they both said at once.

"And he died last summer. Heart attack."

"Oh boy," Stevie said.

"Wait a minute," Susan Carol said. "Someone else must have seen your grade. A dean or something."

"Actually, four people saw it," Graber said. "My mom and dad, and you're right, the dean who was my academic advisor."

"That's three."

Graber nodded. "Right. The fourth was Whiting, our team's faculty advisor."

"Okay," Susan Carol said. "Your parents still have the report card, right?"

"There are no report cards anymore. We get our grades sent by computer. None of us kept my grades from last spring on file. It isn't as if I made the dean's list."

"But that still leaves the dean."

Graber nodded. "Dean Benjamin Wojenski. I've been looking for him all week."

"Looking for him?"

"He retired last summer. I called his old secretary; I called the alumni office; I called the dean of students' office; I even called the president's office."

"And?"

"They all said the same thing. Can't give out personal information on a member of the faculty or even an ex-member of the faculty. Of course I couldn't tell them why I need to find him, and that probably didn't help. I finally got them all to agree to contact him and give him my numbers."

"And you haven't heard from him?" Susan Carol asked.

"Not a word. Which, if they did contact him, is strange because my dad has known him for about twenty years."

"But your dad has only been at Minnesota State for six years," Stevie said.

"Yeah, I know. But a long time ago he was an assistant coach and then the head coach at Davidson. Wojenski was an English professor there and a big basketball fan. We lost track of him when my dad left Davidson to take the job at DePaul. But when he got hired at MSU, there was Wojenski, only now he was a dean."

"You think that's all coincidence?" Susan Carol asked.

"All I know is, I haven't been able to find him. I even put in a call to the alumni office at Davidson. Someone there actually called me back and left a message saying she might be able to help, but I haven't heard from her since, and when I try to call, I get voice mail."

"What's her name?" Susan Carol asked, producing a notebook suddenly.

Graber shrugged. "I don't know what good it will do, but her name's Christine Braman. Her office number's 704-555-4190. I know it by heart at this point."

"Did you try to get a home number?" Susan Carol asked.

"Yeah, I did," Graber said. "There was no one named Braman in the phone book anywhere near Davidson. But if she had any information for me, she would have it at the office."

"Makes sense. So, what happened Monday morning with Whiting?" Stevie asked, bringing him back to his story.

"Oh yeah, I got kind of sidetracked, didn't I?" He looked at his watch. Stevie looked at his. It was 11:20.

"Okay, so Whiting tells me there's this problem with my transcript from the spring. To tell the truth, I'm not that upset at first, I figure it's just a mistake and he, as the team's faculty advisor, is here to help straighten it out. But then Whiting says there's no mistake.

"I ask him what the hell he's talking about. And he says to me, '*And* you also flunked a course in the fall. Which means you were ineligible to play both semesters. Add that up and you're looking at causing the school to forfeit every game it won this year, the conference title, making the Final Four, not to mention facing a serious NCAA investigation because your dad knowingly used an ineligible player.'

"I say, 'Slow down. I didn't flunk a course this fall.' That's when he produced another transcript. And this transcript shows I did flunk a course."

"Which one?" Stevie asked.

"Why don't you take a wild guess," Chip said.

Stevie and Susan Carol looked at one another. They got the answer at the exact same moment: "Ethics and Morals . . ."

"In American Society Today," Chip said, finishing the sentence for them. "Taught by Thomas R. Whiting. I got a B in that damn class, a legitimate B, not one of those Bs I get sometimes because the prof loves hoops. He hands me this transcript and it's got a big fat F for a grade in Ethics and Morals."

"Which is when you knew he was blackmailing you," Stevie said.

"It's when I knew something was rotten in Denmark."

"Denmark?" Stevie said.

"*Hamlet*," Susan Carol said. "You haven't read *Hamlet*?"

Stevie felt himself redden a little bit.

"Even I've read *Hamlet*," Chip said. "The Cliffs Notes anyway. Point is, I knew he was up to no good. I handed him back the transcript and I said, 'What's this all about?' That's when he told me we have to get to the championship game, and then we have to lose. Otherwise these false transcripts will be made public and there's no way for me to prove they're false. He's got documentation. I've got nothing."

"And you're pretty convinced he isn't in this alone?" It was Susan Carol who asked. Stevie had been wondering about that, too.

"He's fronting for others, I'm sure. When I said something about it being his word against mine and my dad's if he went public, he just smiled and said, 'Trust me, Chip, that won't be the case.' I suppose he could be bluffing, but I don't think so. For one thing, he'd probably need help from someone to break into the computer system and make the changes in my grades."

"A computer whiz?"

"Or someone pretty high up. For all his fancy titles, he's still just a faculty member."

"What does your dad think about all this?" Stevie asked.

Chip shook his head. "Nothing. I haven't told him. It would ruin the biggest week of his life. And he can't do any more than I can. If he comes out and says I didn't flunk those courses, he just looks like a coach covering up *and* a father covering up. Double whammy."

"Which means the best hope is finding Dean Wojenski," Susan Carol said.

"Even that's no sure thing. I'm sure he sees a lot of transcripts. If he's retired, who's to say he's got his records with him or even has access to them back at school."

"Still, he may be our only hope," Stevie said.

"*Our* hope?" Chip said, laughing. "You an MSU fan, Steve?"

Stevie reddened even more than he had after his *Hamlet* blunder. "No, but I don't want to see them get away with this," he said.

"Well, my friend," Chip Graber said, "on that we can agree."

11: MAKING PLANS

IT WAS GETTING CLOSE TO NOON, and Chip had to get to his walk-through with the team, so they decided to do some quick planning.

"What I really want to do is win tonight and *then* worry about Monday," Chip said. "I have to believe there's a way for us to win the national championship without Whiting ruining everything."

"If they did go public, it wouldn't just affect MSU, would it?" Susan Carol said. "It would probably hurt your pro career, too."

Chip smiled. "That's the one thing it probably wouldn't affect. The NBA couldn't care less if you were ineligible, if you flunked out of school, if you broke the law, or if you're mean to little old ladies and children. Those guys only care if you can win games. But it would affect my marketing. I've already got people lining up to pay me to sell their products. If it came out that my dad and I somehow conspired to keep me on the court when I was ineligible, that would come to a screeching halt.

"But that isn't what this is about. This is about right and wrong. I'm not a cheat and neither is my father, and these sleazebags are trying to make some kind of killing betting on a game or else *we'll* be the ones people think are bad guys."

The plan they concocted before Chip had to go downstairs was fairly simple: Susan Carol and Stevie would track down the woman at Davidson who had at least said she would try to help Chip find Wojenski. Susan Carol, naturally, knew all about Davidson. "It's a very good school with a great basketball history," she said. "They play Duke every year."

Stevie resisted the urge to make a smart remark about the importance of playing Duke. Especially since Susan Carol had a good plan: If there was no answer in Christine Braman's office (likely), call the campus police and say there was an emergency and could they help them get in touch with her right away.

"Should have thought of that myself," Chip said.

"You've had a lot on your mind," Susan Carol said.

If Christine Braman couldn't help, they would go back to the Minnesota State angle. Chip gave them several names of faculty members he thought might have been friendly enough with Wojenski to have some idea where he now lived. The key, they decided, was finding a number for

Wojenski by tomorrow, when the plot would be in play if MSU won tonight.

Stevie came up with the idea of trying to track down Chip's Econ professor's family. He might have died, but his school records could still be around.

"We'll do what we can this afternoon," Susan Carol said. "If you guys win tonight, we should probably make plans to talk tomorrow."

"Let me give you my cell phone number," he said. "It will be crazy in the locker room after the game, and we may not get a chance to talk. If we don't, call me on the cell."

He walked them to the door. There was no sign of Mike the Giant in the hallway. They wished him luck in the game and he nodded gravely. They were halfway down the hall when Stevie heard a door open behind them.

"Hey, guys," Graber called softly. They turned and he said, "I forgot to say thanks. Whatever happens, thanks."

"Thank us when this is all over," Stevie said.

"I will," he said. "But thanks now." He waved and shut the door.

Stevie looked at Susan Carol. "We've got to get him out of this."

■ ■ ■

They were going to take a cab back to the Hyatt to save time, but there was a line of people waiting for cabs, so they started walking toward the Hilton, hoping to catch another shuttle bus. Stevie wished he had won the argument with his dad about a cell phone. "We're not that late," Stevie said.

"No, but my dad doesn't like me to be late at all," Susan Carol said. "He worries."

It was twelve-forty-five when they walked into the Hyatt lobby. Not surprisingly, both fathers were standing there waiting for them.

"Where in the world have you two been?" Bill Thomas said. "We had you paged in the lobby at the Hilton. We were about to come over there and look for you."

Reverend Thomas gave Susan Carol a hug and then a look. "First, tell me you're okay," he said. "Then tell me why you're so late."

"We're okay," Susan Carol said. "It just got kind of crazy over there. When we finished the two shows we were asked to do, there were all these other radio people asking us to go on. We were finished by eleven-fifteen but we were both starving. We thought we would get a quick hamburger and still be back here at noon. But the service in that place was *so* slow."

"And then we couldn't get a cab," Stevie said, adding the one element of truth to the story.

"I'm finally convinced. I'm getting you a cell phone," Reverend Anderson said to Susan Carol.

Seeing an opening, Stevie said, "I could use one, too, Dad."

"Mm-hmm. I'm still not convinced," his dad said.

"Well, Mr. Thomas and I haven't eaten and I need to get moving here," Reverend Anderson said. "You kids can come in and sit with us while we eat. Did you have dessert?"

"Actually, Dad, we never ate," Susan Carol said. "The service was so bad we got up and left. We're starved, too."

Boy, she's good, Stevie thought. She talks us out of the corner, keeps us from missing lunch, *and* gets herself a cell phone.

They all proceeded into the restaurant, which was packed. "This is how it was at the Hilton," Susan Carol said when they were finally seated after a fifteen-minute wait.

Stevie couldn't believe how crowded every place in town was. His dad did a smart thing when they sat down, telling the hostess they wanted to order right away because they were rushed.

"Everyone's rushed," the hostess said.

"These two kids have an interview with CBS in a little while," Reverend Anderson said. Stevie was impressed: a minister lying to get something done. Apparently it ran in the family. Plus, it was a good lie. The hostess's eyes sparked at the mention of CBS.

"Really?" she said. "TV?" She pulled a pad from her pocket. "Why don't I just take your order now—that'll save you time."

After she was gone, Reverend Anderson said, "I feel badly doing that, but the one thing I learned in my years working with the Panthers is that most people will crawl through mud to be on TV, and the rest will help you find the mud just to be associated with TV. It's like a magic trick. Mention TV and all obstacles disappear."

While they were eating, Dick Weiss, who had apparently been sitting on the other side of the restaurant, walked over to the table. "Steve, I left you a message in the room," he said. "We're going to walk over about two-thirty if you want to go with us."

Stevie looked at Susan Carol to see if she thought that was a good idea or if they needed that time to work on their own.

"Is Mr. Brill going then, too?" she asked.

"Absolutely," Weiss said. "I think he left you a message, too."

"Sounds good to me," she said.

Weiss nodded. "Let's meet here on this level just like yesterday," he said.

They finished lunch by one-forty-five and Reverend Anderson glanced at his watch as he signed for his portion of the bill. "I've got just enough time to walk over to the church," he said. He looked at his daughter. "I can trust you to stay out of trouble this afternoon and tonight, can't I?" he said.

She smiled. "Of course, Daddy. Steve and I both have to do stories, so I won't be back until late. But we'll make sure a grown-up walks us back here."

"Good," he said. "You have your key, right?" He stood up and kissed his daughter on the forehead.

The hostess was back. "You folks get everything okay?" she said. They all told her she had been wonderful, and she looked at Stevie and Susan Carol and said, "Now, when you see Jim Nantz, you tell him when he gets tired of Bonnie Bernstein, he needs to call Jan Miley, right here at the Hyatt. I did TV work in college, and I am ready."

Stevie hadn't really noticed before but she was pretty,

tall, and blond. He imagined there were probably thousands of Jan Mileys in the world who wanted to replace Bonnie Bernstein as CBS's on-court reporter at the Final Four.

"We'll make sure to pass the message to Jim," Bill Thomas said.

As she walked away, he shook his head and laughed. "Don was right. Mention TV to people and it's like waving a magic wand."

Reverend Anderson headed down the escalator to go to his meeting. Susan Carol and Stevie and his dad walked to the elevator. "I'm going to make that call before we go over to the game," Susan Carol said to him as they stepped on the elevator.

"What call is that?" Bill Thomas said.

As usual, Susan Carol covered. "Oh, we wanted to double-check the deadline for tonight with our editor. So I'll do that and then meet you in the lobby, okay, Stevie?"

He wasn't sure how he felt about the fact that she was starting to call him Stevie. But since he messed up and introduced himself that way so often, she probably thought he preferred it. "Sounds good," he said as they got off the elevator. "Let me know what he says."

When they got to the room, Stevie's dad announced he was going to take a shower and then do a little more pregame sightseeing once "all you media types head over to the arena."

He asked Stevie what time the first game started.

"Five-oh-seven," Stevie told him. "Six-oh-seven in the

East." Saying it reminded him there were actually *games* to be played in a few hours.

"Well, let's hope St. Joe's can do it," said his dad. "MSU will be tough."

"Yeah, right," Stevie answered. He felt guilty, realizing he was probably going to be rooting against the team from Philadelphia.

His dad went into the bathroom and Stevie changed his clothes. He was putting his credential around his neck when the phone rang. He looked at his watch. It was 2:25. Maybe Dick Weiss was getting antsy. He picked up the phone on the second ring.

"I may have something." It was Susan Carol.

"What?"

"I found Christine Braman. At least I found her home phone number. She's not home right now, but I'll call her back again when we get to the arena."

"Campus police?"

"No. Didn't have to call them. It's better than that. I'll tell you when we get over there."

"Okay. I'll see you in five minutes."

Stevie's dad had walked out of the bathroom with a towel around his waist. "Who was that?" he asked.

"Oh. Mr Weiss. I guess he wants to get going. I told him I'd be right down."

Bill Thomas nodded. "The game doesn't start for almost three hours. It's a five-minute walk over there, and he's itchy to get going."

"Guess that's why they call him Hoops."

"Guess so." His dad looked at him for a moment and smiled. Then he put both hands on his shoulders. "I'm not sure I've told you how proud I am of you," he said.

Stevie felt himself flush a little bit. "Gee, Dad, what'd I do?"

"You won the contest. You're writing stories like a real pro this weekend. And you've handled yourself very well. I think even Susan Carol is coming around. I heard her call you Stevie."

"Come on, Dad."

"Okay, you go. Have a great time. Just remember I'm proud of you."

"Thanks, Dad."

As he gently shut the door behind him, he couldn't help but wonder if what he had done that morning would make his dad proud, too.

All he could do was hope.

■ ■ ■

The walk over to the Superdome was a little bit like taking in all the sideshow acts at a circus at once. Stevie was convinced he saw a bearded lady at one point. There were several fortune-tellers, not to mention all the various ticket-scalpers and vendors selling "official" merchandise. Stevie looked around for Big Tex, but he was nowhere in sight. Stevie wondered for a moment if maybe Big Tex had been arrested. Unlikely, he thought.

They made it through security with relatively little hassle, helped by the fact that they were early and that they didn't have to pick up credentials. The NCAA guy who had kept demanding Stevie's driver's license the previous day was still there, but he didn't even look at Stevie or Weiss as they walked through the metal detectors. Once inside, they all headed straight to the workroom to set up their computers near telephones.

"I think we should walk out courtside," Susan Carol said to Stevie once they had plugged their computers in and checked to make sure the electricity was working.

"Nothing going on out there right now," Bill Brill said. "The teams probably aren't even in the building yet. It's only three o'clock."

"Yeah, I know," said Susan Carol. "But I kind of want to see the place fill up. For my story."

That seemed to satisfy Brill. The two of them walked out to the arena floor, where the giant screens in each corner of the building were showing a replay of the 2004 final between Connecticut and Georgia Tech. Stevie remembered falling asleep at halftime with UConn in complete control.

"Duke should have been in that game, not Connecticut," Susan Carol said.

"I know, I know. J.J. Redick got fouled on the last play."

"Well, as a matter of fact, he was, but the worst call was on the play before when Emeka Okafor went over Luol Deng's back for that offensive rebound."

Stevie *did* recall thinking the same thing, but he wasn't about to admit it. "Well, Okafor won't be out there tonight," he said.

"Neither will Deng—and he *should* be. It's crazy to go pro after one year of college."

Stevie didn't answer because they had arrived on press row. There were very few people around. A couple of reporters at their seats writing pregame stories. And he could see Jim Nantz and Billy Packer standing near their seats with a coterie of people around them.

"Think I should go tell Nantz about Jan Miley?" he said.

"What? Who? Oh, the hostess. Absolutely. I'm sure Bonnie Bernstein will be quaking in her pumps."

They sat down in an open area and Susan Carol glanced around at the empty building, partly for her story, but mostly to make sure no one could hear them. The fans had not yet been let in, so there were no more than 200 people—including all the ushers—in a place that would soon hold 65,000. Stevie liked the emptiness.

Susan Carol took another look around to be absolutely certain no one could hear them. "So, first I tried to find Chip's Econ professor's family, which was dead easy. His widow is still in Rochester—she was the only Scott in town. Plus, she was home. But that's where our luck ran out. Professor Scott never kept any records at home, and his wife seemed sure they would have cleaned out his office at the college.

"But *then* I called this Braman woman's number," she said, "and I got voice mail."

"Figures, on a Saturday—"

She put up a hand to stop him. "Right. And I'm about to hang up, because there's no sense leaving a message, when I hear the tape say, 'If this is Chip, *please* call me at home. My number is'"—she paused to pull out her notebook—"'704-555-2346.'"

"Wow! So did you call?"

She nodded. "Yeah. And get this: she wasn't home but her tape said, 'Chip, if it's you, either leave me a number where I can find you or call me back after four o'clock. I know you play at six, but I have that information you needed.'"

Stevie looked up at the giant digital clock on the scoreboard. It said 3:14. He noticed that fans were now starting to make their way into seats.

"So we have to wait another forty-five minutes and call back," Susan Carol said.

"But we aren't Chip," Stevie said. "What are we going to—" He stopped himself in mid-sentence, suddenly struck by the last words on Christine Braman's tape: *You play at six*.

"Hey, wait a minute," he said. "She's in Charlotte. That means she's on eastern time, which means it's four-fifteen already. We need to call her now."

Susan Carol smacked her fist lightly on the table in front of her. "I completely forgot," she said. "How dumb am I? We've got to find a phone."

"Preferably one with some privacy," he said.

"Good point," she said.

They were sitting at three seats that were all marked THE WASHINGTON POST. There was a phone that also said WASHINGTON POST on it sitting just to Stevie's right. No one was anywhere near them.

"This might be as good a place as any," he said. "It's a zoo back there in the press room."

"I wonder if I can call long-distance from here," she said.

Stevie looked around. There was no one looking at them, and the closest people to them were the CBS types who were two rows and almost half the court away. "I don't think one long-distance call is going to kill the *Washington Post*," he said.

She nodded and opened her notebook again to the phone number. "Keep an eye out and nudge me if you see someone coming," she said.

Stevie played guard for the next few minutes, walking up and down behind Susan Carol while she talked. He couldn't hear exactly what she was saying, because she was practically whispering into the phone, but she was taking a lot of notes and there were periods where she just listened and wrote. He did hear her say one thing that baffled him: "Oh, I'm adopted."

No one came near them the entire time she was on the phone, which was a relief because he wasn't sure what he would have said. After about ten minutes, she hung up. It had felt more like ten hours. She was clearly excited.

"Any luck?" he said, pretty certain she had at least had some.

"Yes, big time, I think," she said. "She apparently transposed two numbers on Chip's cell phone and couldn't reach him. That's why she left him that message on her phone at work."

"Nice. Does she have a phone number for Wojenski?"

"Better than that. She told me he's living in Mississippi in a place called Bay St. Louis."

"Why have I heard of that place?"

"Because the local radio guy who was the MC at the breakfast yesterday said he lived there."

"That's right," Stevie said. "He said he lived an hour and a lifetime from downtown New Orleans."

"Ms. Braman said she was sure the dean wouldn't mind her giving me his number and address."

"Why did I hear you say something about being adopted?"

"Oh, yeah. I told her that I was Chip's sister. She said she thought she had read that Chip was an only child. That was the best I could come up with."

"Quick thinking there."

She was staring at the number she had written down in her notebook.

"I know we need to call him," she said. "But we may have caught a lucky break with him living so close. I figured he would be retired to Florida or someplace like that. If he's this close, I think we should try to see him in person."

"Journalism 101," Stevie said, remembering another of Jerardi's lessons. "Always interview in person whenever you can."

Susan Carol smiled. "Right. Especially when a lot is at stake." Her smile disappeared. "You know, you and I may never work on a bigger story than this one."

Stevie felt a slight chill run through him. He knew there was a lot more at stake than the story. "Now all we have to do," he said, "is figure out how to get to Bay St. Louis, Mississippi."

12: BUZZER BEATER

OF COURSE, before they figured out how to get to Bay St. Louis, they had to call Dean Wojenski and make sure he was willing and able to help. They didn't really have much yet, but it still felt like a victory. By now the building was starting to fill up with people, and the St. Joe's fans, who were directly behind the spot on press row where Stevie and Susan Carol were sitting, were exchanging cheers and insults with the Minnesota State fans, who were diagonally across the court from them. The two sections that Stevie guessed were for the Connecticut and Duke fans were still almost empty. Stevie could feel a buzz replacing the quiet that he had enjoyed when they first walked onto the court.

Susan Carol was about to dial Dean Wojenski's number, when Stevie noticed Tony Kornheiser walking toward him, along with his TV partner, Michael Wilbon. He knew they both worked for the *Washington Post* when they weren't doing their show, *Pardon the Interruption*, which was the only ESPN show Stevie watched. Every other show on the network was filled with shouting that, unlike Vitale's good-natured shouting, had a nasty, angry edge.

"Put down the phone," he said to Susan Carol. He jumped up and, as Kornheiser got close to him, said, "Did you ever get your suite, Mr. Kornheiser?"

Kornheiser looked at him for a moment as if he were from the moon. Then recognition registered on his face. "You're the kid who was in the lobby the other night, right? You and your dad."

"Right," Stevie said. He put out his hand. "I'm Steve Thomas." He turned to Susan Carol and said, "This is Susan Carol Anderson. We were the winners of the USBWA writing contest. That's why we have"—he held up his credential as if Kornheiser couldn't see it unless he did—"press passes."

"Well, good for you," Kornheiser said, shaking hands with him as Susan Carol stood up to shake hands, too. "Hey, Wilbon, here are a couple of real journalists, not talking heads like you and me."

Wilbon was a lot taller than Stevie had imagined, probably about six foot three. His head was completely shaved, à la Michael Jordan, his self-confessed hero and role model in all things. Stevie remembered something Wilbon had written once when Jordan was still *the* star player in the NBA. Wilbon's wife had complained during a play-off game, "You love Michael more than you love me." To which Wilbon had supposedly replied, "But I love you more than Scottie," a reference to Jordan's Chicago Bulls sidekick, Scottie Pippen.

"Nice to meet you guys," he said, shaking hands. He looked at both of them, pointed at Susan Carol, and said, "Let me guess: high school senior," then, turning to Stevie, "high school sophomore."

Stevie immediately liked him for thinking he was a sophomore. "I'll bet you they're both younger than that," Kornheiser said. "First, you're just sucking up to Stevie the way you always suck up to people when you meet them, because he's no more than a freshman, probably an eighth grader." He pointed at Susan Carol. "She's tougher because she's tall and because girls always look older. You know what? I say they're both eighth graders."

Wilbon laughed. "You're crazy. She's an eighth grader? No way."

"I'm an eighth grader," Susan Carol said.

"No you're not," Wilbon answered.

Kornheiser threw his hands into the air. "What are you, her father? You know how old she is, and she doesn't know how old she is?"

"Right," Wilbon said.

Stevie and Susan Carol were both laughing now. They were getting a real-life version of *PTI*, live and undoctored by tape or a producer.

Kornheiser and Wilbon were also laughing. Susan Carol said, "Listen, if I can prove to you that I'm really thirteen, can I use your phone for five minutes?"

"You can use our phone for as long as you want, no matter how old you are," Wilbon said. "But you're seventeen, trust me." He put his computer down and walked by them to say hello to some other people farther down the row.

"Right. And you and I are thirty-nine," Kornheiser said to Wilbon's back as he left. He plunked his computer down on the table and looked at Stevie. "Can you believe I have to write live tonight? That's not what I do. I'm not a writer anymore, I'm a yodeler."

"They must not know who you are."

Kornheiser patted him on the back. "Kid, you've got a future." He pointed at Susan Carol. "If you're smart, you stick with her. Because she *definitely* has a future. We need more women in sports."

"She really is thirteen."

"I know. Here's the difference between Wilbon and me. I have a twenty-year-old daughter. I remember what she looked like at thirteen. He has no daughters and no clue."

The fans were screaming Kornheiser's name. He sighed. "This is why I hate being out in public," he said. "Do you hear that? What am I supposed to do? Ignore them? I can't do that. I have to go sign."

"You have a very hard life, don't you?" Stevie said.

"Son, you don't know the half of it," he said, and went off to pay the price for his fame by signing autographs.

As soon as they were gone, Susan Carol sat back down at the *Post* phone. It was getting louder in the building with each passing minute. To their right, the St. Joe's band was filing into their seats in the end zone. "Better call right now," he said. "It's going to be impossible to hear soon."

She was already dialing. "Dean Wojenski?" he heard her say a moment later. "I think you heard from Ms. Braman at Davidson about Chip Graber trying to track you down?"

Stevie didn't try to eavesdrop on the rest of the conversation. The band was starting to warm up and Susan Carol had to put a hand over her open ear as she talked. The last thing Stevie heard her do was give the doctor what sounded like an e-mail address: "It's SCDevil@aol.com," he heard her say.

She hung up. The band was now playing the St. Joe's fight song full force. "Let's go in back," she shouted.

"Is he going to help?" he shouted back.

She nodded and pointed toward the tunnel. They stopped in the hallway, which was filled with people walking to and from the floor.

"He wants us to come out and see him tomorrow," she said quietly when they found a spot where they could lean against the wall out of the way of all the traffic. "He said if Chip's in trouble, he wants to help."

"How in the world are we going to get there?" he said.

"I told him that might be a problem," she said. "He said he didn't want to come into New Orleans unless he absolutely had to. I said we would figure something out."

"What did you tell him?"

"I told him that Chip had a serious problem and it was related to his transcript from last spring," she said. "He said that Chip had always been a borderline student, but as far as he knew he was on probation but okay to play at the end of last year. I told him someone had doctored Chip's transcript after he retired. That's when he said we should come to the house. He said he still had lots of MSU stuff in files and that he'd look to see if he had his student records from last year. He suggested that if there was any way for Chip to come, he should be there, too."

"Well, if they lose this game, Chip will have plenty of time tomorrow. And *he* can drive a car."

"I think he'll make the time one way or the other. This could be solid proof. Wojenski said he would e-mail me directions. He said it's just about sixty miles from here to his house."

That was what the e-mail address was about. "SCDevil?" he asked.

She didn't even blush a little. "Don't start," she said.

Stevie had one more thought. "Did you tell him you were Chip's sister?"

"Uh-huh."

"Wouldn't he know Chip's an only child?"

"You know, that's a good point," she said. "It never came up."

■ ■ ■

The rest of the evening passed Stevie like a train flashing by on a high-speed railroad track. Once the games began, it was all a blur. He and Susan Carol had much better seats than he had dared hope. They were in the second row of what was called overflow media, which meant they were sitting in the second row in the stands, just behind the three rows of press seating. Most of the other overflow media were reporters and producers from the local TV stations in each of the four towns where the teams were from. But there were some media celebrities, too, including Chris Wallace from Fox News, who was sitting right next to Susan Carol.

Susan Carol asked what he was doing at the Final Four. "We're doing the show from here tomorrow," he said. "We have a panel that's going to discuss what's wrong with college athletics."

"I hope your show is at least four hours long," Stevie said, realizing he had become a true cynic in just a couple of days.

"You aren't the first person to say something like that," Wallace said.

"Who's on the panel?" Susan Carol asked.

"It's an interesting group," Wallace said. "We have Tom Izzo, the coach at Michigan State, and Roy Williams, the coach at North Carolina, to talk from the coaches' point of view. Then, to talk about it from the academic side, we have the outgoing president of Duke—"

"Dr. Sanford?" Susan Carol said.

"Yes, good man, I think," Wallace said. "I like the fact that he said he wants to retire and go back to teaching because he's tired of being a glorified fund-raiser. And our fourth panelist is the faculty representative at Minnesota State, who is some kind of ethics expert."

They both went wide-eyed. "Whiting?" Susan Carol said. "Thomas Whiting?"

"Yes. Why? You know him?"

"No, not really. I just know he's close to Chip Graber."

"Oh, I didn't know that. We actually tried to get Koheen, the MSU president, too, but they said he had to go to a fund-raising brunch."

"Guess Dr. Sanford is right," Stevie said.

"Oh, he's right," Wallace said. "There's no doubt he's right."

They sat back in their seats to watch the game. Stevie couldn't believe how the place had filled up. He looked up at the seats in the upper deck and saw they were completely full. Somewhere up there was his dad. "The players must look like ants from up in the top deck," he commented to Susan Carol, thinking how lucky they were.

Everything about the Final Four was big. The PA was *loud*, and the announcer seemed to take several days introducing the players. The TV time-outs seemed to last forever, no doubt because he couldn't click to something else during the three minutes of commercials he knew CBS was showing.

The game itself was intense, right from the start. Each team had a great guard whom the coaches built their offense around: Graber for MSU, Tommy Watson for the Hawks. Early on, St. Joe's got several long threes from senior Pat Carroll, a skinny guy. Stevie thought he could be just like if not for the fact that Carroll was six foot five. But MSU was dominating under the net—sucking up every rebound. At halftime it was 33–30, St. Joe's, and Stevie realized that he was pulling for Minnesota State, which would have been unthinkable twenty-four hours earlier. Graber had 15 of his team's 30 points. Whiting couldn't accuse him of not trying.

When they got out of their seats at halftime, Stevie could barely walk—he must have had every muscle tensed while he was watching. He wasn't sure if he'd even blinked in the last hour. They went to the press room for something to drink and to pick up statistics sheets. It occurred to Stevie that he hadn't given even a little thought to what he might write. He was supposed to write some kind of feature off the first game, and Susan Carol would cover the second game.

On the way back to their seats—there was plenty of time, since the halftimes were stretched out to twenty minutes so CBS could get in still more commercials—Stevie and Susan Carol walked past the radio locations on the third row. As they did, Stevie noticed someone staring at them. "Uh-oh," he said. It was their friend from the hotel, Jerry Ventura. Clearly, he had recognized them, and, just as clearly, he was wondering what they were doing wearing press credentials. Susan Carol started to stop, but Stevie gave her a little shove to keep her walking. "I'll tell you when we get to the seats," he hissed.

When he told her about Ventura, she said, "You're sure he saw us?"

"Positive."

"We should have thought about that," she said.

"We can avoid him," he said.

"Not once this game is over. We better come up with a story."

"That's your department, Scarlett," he said.

She laughed. "Easy for you to say. Well, I've got the second half to think of something."

As it turned out, she had the second half and a five-minute overtime. St. Joe's raced to a 10-point lead early in the second half, but then Graber really heated up. Everything in the MSU offense seemed geared to getting him shots. "Nice double-post," Susan Carol said at one stage, pointing to two Purple Tide players out near the foul line. Their job was to set screens for Graber so he could get open shots before the defenders reached him.

"Yeah—St. Joe's can't get to Chip because he's got such a quick release," Stevie said.

A three pointer by Graber, which gave him 30 points for the night, tied the score at 67 with 2:12 to go, and the teams seesawed to the finish, trading baskets until a Watson jumper just before the buzzer tied the score at 75–75 and sent the game into overtime. The overtime was even more tense than regulation, if that was possible. Five minutes seemed to take five hours. Stevie looked at his watch. It was 7:50. The game had been going on for nearly three hours. With eleven seconds left, Graber, double-teamed, fed his center, Tammu Abate, for an open dunk that put MSU up, 83–82. Since St. Joe's was out of time-outs, Watson came straight downcourt with the ball, drove the middle, and, as the defense collapsed on him, pitched the ball to Carroll, who buried a three to put them up 85–83 with 3.9 seconds on the clock. MSU called time-out.

"If they lose, they certainly can't say Chip didn't give a hundred percent," Susan Carol said to Stevie over the din, which, between the blaring bands and the screeching fans, was earsplitting. Everyone was on their feet.

"Who knows what they'll say," Stevie said. "It's a sure thing he'll take the last shot. If he misses . . ."

She put a hand on his shoulder as if to say the thought scared her. It scared Stevie, too. The teams lined up, and, sure enough, Graber circled back to take the inbounds pass, turned, and sprinted up the court with Watson all over him and two defenders coming to meet him. He cut to the right to try to clear some space and, still thirty-five feet from the basket, he pulled up as the clock hit one second. He was leaning to his right to get the ball off over Watson's lunge, and as he released it, Stevie heard the buzzer go off. For an instant, everything seemed to go slo-mo as Stevie watched the ball arc toward the basket. He wasn't sure why, but he knew it was going to go in. Then it looked as if he was wrong. The ball hit the backboard, bounced off it, and hit the front rim. The whole building held its breath. It hung on the rim for, Stevie guessed, an hour or so. Finally, it dropped into the basket.

Never in his life had Stevie heard anything so loud. The place simply exploded with sound. Stevie found himself jumping up and down, hugging Susan Carol, which, if anyone had been paying attention to them, would have seemed awfully strange: the kid from Philadelphia hugging the kid from North Carolina because someone from Minnesota had hit a miraculous three-point shot at the buzzer to beat the team from Philly. Fortunately, no one was watching. Midway through the hug, Stevie realized what he was doing and awkwardly let go of Susan Carol.

"Sorry," he screamed.

She didn't answer. There was a wild celebration on the floor as Graber's teammates piled on top of him. Stevie couldn't help but look at Watson and Carroll, both of whom were sitting on the floor, watching in disbelief. Watson was almost on the spot where Graber had released the ball, having lunged at him as he shot. The Minnesota State band tried to storm the court, but they were turned back by security people, who appeared miraculously as soon as Graber's shot went in.

Susan Carol was shouting at him over the noise. He couldn't hear her. She leaned in close. "Now we have no choice," she said. "We have to get Chip out to see Dean Wojenski."

She was right. This game was over. But a far more dangerous one was now under way.

■ ■ ■

The second game was anticlimactic. It was almost halftime by the time Stevie finished writing his story on the first game. Knowing that the Associated Press would fully cover all the details of the play-by-play and of Graber's winning shot, he decided to write about the losers. He had never been in a more quiet place than the St. Joe's locker room. The players handled themselves with amazing grace under the circumstances, answering everyone's questions. So did Coach Phil Martelli. Stevie felt awful for them. He wondered if the other writers felt awful for them, too. As he was standing in a small circle around Tommy Watson's locker, he felt someone nudge him.

He looked up and saw Dick Jerardi, whom he hadn't seen all weekend because he'd been assigned to stay with St. Joe's every step of the way. "This is when the job is really hard," Jerardi said softly. "No one deserves to lose like this. Especially a group of good kids like these guys. I feel terrible for them."

"But we still have a job to do, right?" Stevie said quietly.

"Exactly right," Jerardi said. "Their job is to talk no matter how much it hurts, and our job is to ask the questions and write the story—no matter how much it hurts."

Stevie wrote, filed, and headed back to the court. When he reached press row, there were just under four minutes left in the half and Duke led 45–33, which was a surprise.

"I think they want to get even for last year," Susan Carol said.

"We'll see if it lasts," Stevie said. He wondered again if there was any significance to Whiting's comment to Chip Graber about MSU playing Duke in the final.

It lasted. Connecticut cut the lead to 7 at one point in the second half, but J.J. Redick hit back-to-back three pointers to boost the lead back to 13, and Krzyzewski spread the floor, forcing UConn to foul in the last five minutes. Stevie expected Susan Carol to be ecstatic every time Duke hit a shot. If she was, she didn't show it. When Connecticut made its run, if it made her nervous, he didn't see it. She sat calmly taking notes. When Duke built the lead to 15 with 3:43 left, she turned to Stevie and said, "I'll bet Chip's back at the hotel by now."

In the mayhem after the game, they had decided that

trying to get to Chip in the Dome would be impossible. He had to do a postgame CBS interview, then go to the interview room, where he and his teammates would be called "student-athletes" fourteen times, and then he would be completely surrounded in the locker room until the room was cleared of media. Since Susan Carol had to write after the second game, Stevie would try to reach Chip, fill him in on the good news, and see what his schedule was for the next day.

Stevie checked his watch and nodded. It was after ten. Chip might be free to answer his phone now. He stood up during the TV time-out, picked his way through the seats to press row, which was half empty now because some people were still writing off the first game and others had headed back to start writing the second game, since it appeared unlikely UConn was going to rally. Stevie worked his way to the aisle and headed for the tunnel. He had just reached the top of the ramp when he felt a hand on his shoulder. He turned around with a smile on his face, expecting to see Weiss or Brill or perhaps Jerardi.

"You and I need to have a chat, kid," Jerry Ventura said. "Let's go for a little walk."

13: NEXT STOP, BAY ST. LOUIS

VENTURA KEPT A FIRM GRIP on Stevie's arm as he steered him to the left at the top of the ramp. The press room was to the right. As far as Stevie could see, there was nothing in the direction Ventura was steering him. There were dark curtains on either side of them and a lone sign that said TECHNICAL SERVICES with an arrow pointing down the dark hallway. A runner, carrying stat sheets, walked quickly past without so much as a glance in their direction. Stevie wondered if he should scream for help. Ventura seemed to read his mind.

"If you try to yell," he said, "I will have you arrested for breaking into my room this morning."

If he was bluffing, it was a good bluff.

"Okay, okay," Stevie said. "I'm not going to yell."

Hearing his own voice made him feel a lot calmer for some reason. "I don't need to yell. What exactly is your problem with me? What are you talking about?"

Ventura's face twisted into a smile that looked more like a snarl. "I'll tell you my problem with you and your pretty friend," he said. "You came at me with a bunch of crap this morning about what big MSU fans you were and how thrilled you would be to meet Mike and Trey and got me to give you my room key," he said. "Now you better tell me who you really are and what the hell you wanted in my room."

Stevie now understood the meaning of the phrase "sweating bullets." He had to think of something fast and, for the first time all weekend, he didn't have Susan Carol to back him up. "We didn't want anything in your room," he said, speaking slowly, trying to stall for time so he could think of something. "We just wanted a soda."

Ventura tightened the grip on his arm. "Don't give me that, kid. Don't make me angrier. And don't make me get Trey back here. Tell me why you and the girl have press passes and what you were up to this morning."

Stevie decided the truth would work as well as any story at this point, if only because it might give him a few extra seconds to think. "Okay, okay," he said. "Let go of my arm and I'll tell you."

Ventura softened his grip but didn't let go. "Talk fast," he said.

"My name's Stevie Thomas," he said, giving away nothing, since it was right there on his credential, assuming

152 ·

Ventura could read. "The girl is Susan Carol Anderson. We both won the USBWA writing contest and—"

"What's the USBWA?" Ventura said.

"United States Basketball Writers Association," Stevie said slowly, still playing for time. "There were two winners."

"And two kids from the same family won?"

He really *was* dumb, Stevie thought. "No," he said. "She's not my sister. I'm not even sure why she said that."

"What were you doing in my room?"

"We weren't in your room," Stevie insisted. "We just went up to the lounge, got a couple of sodas, and came back downstairs."

"You were gone longer than that."

"We stopped to watch *SportsCenter* in the lounge. Vitale was on."

"Vitale's always on. What were you doing?"

"Okay. We wanted to get on a team floor because we were hoping to find people to interview—you know, we wanted a story no one else would have. Look, Mr. Ventura, was something missing from your room? Is that why you think we went in there? I'll take a lie detector test that we never stole anything from your room."

For the first time, Ventura's voice softened a little. "No, nothing was missing. It just looked like stuff had been moved around on my desk when I got back. I didn't think much about it until I saw you kids tonight. Then I remembered the key."

"Had the maid cleaned the room when you got back? Could she have moved stuff?"

"I suppose it's possible," he said. Stevie could feel the anger ebbing out of him. "So, did it work? Did you find your scoop?"

"No, there was no one around. We really did watch Vitale."

"All right, kid, go ahead," Ventura said, finally releasing his arm. "But I'm going to check your USBWA story out, and if it's not true, I'll find you again. I promise."

"You can walk into the press room with me right now and read the press release," Stevie said. "It's sitting right on the front table."

"Get going," Ventura said, almost friendly now. "And stay out of trouble."

"You got it," Stevie said.

Ventura walked back down the hall, leaving Stevie alone in the darkness to catch his breath. That had been close, he thought. Too close.

■ ■ ■

By the time Stevie made it into the press room, the game was just about over. Duke was shooting free throws and the clock was under a minute. He walked to the phone next to his computer. Weiss was sitting nearby writing. He looked up quickly. "Long time no see, kid," he said. "Having fun?"

"Oh yeah," Stevie said. "Just need to use the phone."

"Have at it," Weiss said.

Stevie took out his notebook and found Chip's cell phone number. He turned his back on Weiss, who was clearly focused on what he was writing. Graber answered on the first ring.

"It's Stevie," he said, not wanting to say Graber's name on the off chance someone might hear him.

"Yeah. We're eating right now," Graber said softly. "What's new?" He said it casually, clearly because people were around him.

"Well, first, congratulations. That was amazing."

"Yeah. Very lucky. Thanks."

"Second, we need to talk. We found Wojenski and he's actually near here. He thinks he can help and wants us to come see him."

There was a pause on the other end.

"Oh my God. That's incredible. Okay," Graber said after a few seconds. He dropped his voice even lower. "Let's do this. Meet me on the second floor of my hotel at eight in the morning. Where the radio guys were."

"Um, I don't think I want to run into them again."

"You won't. There won't be anyone around that early. Everyone will sleep in. Can you do it?"

"We'll do it."

"Okay. See you then."

He hung up. Stevie looked up to see people pouring into the press room. The second game had just ended.

Susan Carol arrived with a big smile on her face. Why not? Her team had won.

"Did you get him?" she said quietly when she reached him.

"Yes. He wants us to meet him at eight in the morning on the second floor of his hotel near where we met the radio guys."

"Oooh," she said, cringing slightly. "I don't think I need to see those guys again."

"You don't know the half of it," he said.

"Why? What happened?"

"I'll tell you later. Meantime, we have to figure a way to ditch our dads again tomorrow."

"We'll deal with *that* later. Meantime, I have to get a story written."

"Let me help you," he said. "It will save time. I can go to the interview room, you go to the locker room, or vice versa."

She put a hand on his shoulder. "Thanks. That would help a lot. I want to check out the locker room scene. And I need some interview room quotes from UConn on why they thought Duke was able to control the game so easily. One good quote from Coach Calhoun, maybe one good player quote."

"Done," he said.

They went in different directions and met thirty minutes later back at her computer. He fed her the quotes she wanted and she had the story finished in forty-five minutes. Once again, Dick Weiss was still working. Once again, Bill Brill was finished. "Do you have to do radio?" Stevie asked.

"I have to do about five beers back at the hospitality room in the hotel," Brill said. "Let's go."

It was exactly midnight when they walked out of the building. A steady rain was falling and the walkway from the Dome to the hotel was almost empty. Stevie was glad they had Brill with them.

They were all quite wet by the time they reached the

entrance to the mall that led to the Hyatt, and relieved that it had not been locked. When they reached the hotel, Brill headed to the media hospitality room. Stevie and Susan Carol headed for the elevators. "We need to make a plan for the morning before we go to bed," Stevie said. He could feel the exhaustion in his bones, but he was also buzzing with adrenaline from the day.

They got off on 19, which was Stevie's floor, and decided to talk there. No one was around, at least for the moment. Stevie briefly told Susan Carol what had happened with Ventura. "You think you convinced him?" she said.

"Yeah, I do. It was pretty close to the truth, really."

"Yeah. And we're just a couple of kids," she said. "How much trouble could we be causing?"

"Speaking of trouble, you have any idea how to convince our dads we need to leave the hotel at seven-thirty in the morning?"

"Yes, I do," she said.

He wasn't surprised. "And?"

"There's a Fellowship of Christian Athletes meeting and prayer service at eight-thirty tomorrow morning at the Hilton. I saw it on the schedule they gave my dad. I'll tell him I'm going to go instead of going to church because I'll get a service and maybe get a story on the players who show up."

"What about me? I don't go to church on Sundays."

"Just tell your dad there may be a story there for you because a lot of the coaches attend."

It was a good idea. The time was just about right and he could probably convince his father there was a story there.

"Okay. That sounds good. I'll meet you in the lobby at seven-thirty."

She nodded. She started toward the elevator, then stopped. She walked back to where he was standing, put an arm around his shoulder, leaned down, and brushed a kiss on his cheek. Stevie felt his legs get a little bit weak, and he wondered if he was supposed to do anything in response.

"Um, what was that for?" he said.

"For making me feel safe," she said, turning away. "I'll see you at seven-thirty."

Stevie walked to his room feeling about ten feet tall. Or, at the very least, five foot eight.

■ ■ ■

His dad was lying on the bed reading a magazine when Stevie walked in. "Sorry I'm so late," he said.

"You know, I was actually rethinking that cell phone for a while," his dad said. "But I wasn't really worried. I knew it would be a late night after that first game took so long. You must be tired."

"Yeah," he said. "But can you set the alarm for seven-fifteen?"

His father knitted his eyebrows. "Seven-fifteen? Why so early?"

Stevie sighed as if greatly burdened. "Well, there's this Fellowship of Christian Athletes prayer breakfast at the Hilton, and a lot of big-time guys are supposed to be there. I thought I'd go and get my Sunday story early rather than wait until the afternoon press conferences with the teams."

"A prayer breakfast?"

"Dad, I'm not going to pray, I'm going to report."

"Uh-huh. And will Susan Carol be there, too?"

"Yeah, she's the one who told me about it."

His father smiled in a way that made Stevie blush but refrained from comment. Instead he changed the subject. "Tough night, huh? Amazing finish, but it's too bad St. Joe's lost."

Stevie really wanted to relive the game with his dad, but he was crashing. "It was amazing," he said through a jaw-breaking yawn.

"We'll talk in the morning," said his dad.

■ ■ ■

And then somehow the alarm was going off. Stevie's father hit the snooze button while Stevie groaned and wondered how it could possibly be morning already. He lay perfectly still for a moment, wondering if he could roll over and go back to sleep. Maybe Susan Carol and Chip didn't really need him. Yes they did, he finally thought, and rolled himself out of bed.

Seeing him up, his father turned over to go back to sleep. "Try to be back for lunch, okay?" he mumbled.

Stevie said nothing. He had no idea when he would be back. He pushed himself under the shower, which at least got his eyes open, got dressed, and slipped quietly out the door. His father was sound asleep.

Susan Carol was waiting for him, her hair tied back in a wet ponytail. She was holding a Styrofoam cup.

"Coffee?" he said, surprised.

"I drink it sometimes before morning swim practice when I'm really tired," she said. "It helps."

"You swim?"

She nodded. "Uh-huh. I'm a butterflyer."

They started walking. It was a cool morning and the shuttle buses weren't running yet.

"Doesn't that taste awful?"

"Not with milk and sugar," she said. "Try a sip."

She handed him the cup and he took a tiny sip. The hot liquid felt good going down and it really didn't taste bad. "Pretty good, actually," he said.

"My dad doesn't know I drink it," she said. "He'd be horrified. He says caffeine can be an addiction, too."

The streets of the city were remarkably empty. There were a few people out running and some bleary-eyed tourists. That was about it.

"Looks like everyone is still asleep," Susan Carol said.

"I don't blame them," Stevie answered with a yawn. Susan Carol gave him the last of her coffee.

It was 7:55 when they walked into the Marriott lobby, which was almost deserted. Just them and the security guards.

"You bring the key just in case?" he asked. She pulled it out of her pocket and Stevie felt better. They walked to the escalator unimpeded but Stevie was convinced they were being watched, if only because the security people had nothing better to do. There was another security guard at the top of the escalator. He nodded at Stevie and Susan Carol, who nodded back as casually as possible.

Stevie was relieved to see that the only sign of the MSU

radio network was the banner hanging over the table where they had been broadcasting the day before. Chip Graber was waiting for them, pacing. If Stevie hadn't been expecting him, he might not have recognized him. He wore black sweatpants, a gray sweatshirt that said HOLY CROSS BASKET-BALL, and a blue cap with a Mets orange NY on it. He had the cap pulled down so low on his head you couldn't see his eyes.

"I thought you'd never get here," Graber said. Neither Stevie nor Susan Carol saw much point in telling him they were a couple of minutes early.

"Let's go for a walk," he continued. "I want to put some distance between us and Whiting—or anyone else with the team, really."

"Okay," Susan Carol said, starting to turn back toward the escalator.

"No, no, there's a better way," he said. "Follow me."

He walked them down the wide hallway until they reached an EXIT sign and then down a stairwell that came out on a side street. "First thing I figure out in every hotel is the back way out," he said. "Most of the time, walking through the lobby is murder. Let's head toward Jackson Square. We'll blend in with the tourists."

As they walked down the narrow streets of the French Quarter, Chip pelted them with questions.

"So you talked to Dean Wojenski? And he really thinks he can help? What did he say, how did you find him?"

Susan Carol quickly told him what they had learned and how they had learned it. Graber laughed when she told him that she was now his adopted little sister.

"And he wants us to go to his house?"

"Yes. He said he lives about an hour from here." She pulled a piece of paper out of her pocket. "He e-mailed me directions and I printed them out last night after the game. It's exactly sixty-one miles from here according to the Map-Quest thing he sent me."

"So if we're going, we need a car," Stevie said.

Graber nodded. "That's not a problem," he said. He pulled a cell phone from his pocket, snapped it open, and dialed a number. It was apparently picked up quickly. "Bobby Mo," he said. "Grabes."

There was a pause while Bobby Mo said something. "Yeah, man, thanks. Better to be lucky than good, right?" He listened some more, laughed—a fake laugh if Stevie had ever heard one. "Well, I appreciate it. Listen, you said if I needed something, to call you. I need something." Another pause. "No, no, nothing like that. Come on, I'm playing for the national championship tomorrow night. I need some wheels for a couple of hours. Can you hook me up?"

More talking by Bobby Mo. "Good. No, don't bring it to the Marriott, too many people. We're in Jackson Square. How soon can you be here? Twenty minutes? Okay. There's an outdoor café on the corner—the Café du Monde, it says—meet us there?"

Bobby Mo must have said something in response to the word "us," because Graber laughed. "I've got a couple of my cousins with me. I promised I'd take them for a drive to get away from the crowds."

He snapped the phone closed. "All set."

"Who was that?" Susan Carol asked about a split second before Stevie could.

"His name's Bobby Maurice. He works for Brickley Shoes. All the shoe companies have been sniffing around since I was a sophomore. They all want to sign me because they think I'm 'marketable.' Basically, any of them will do anything I ask them to do, including get me a car for a few hours on twenty minutes' notice."

"Isn't Brickley the company that had that big scandal a few years ago?" Stevie asked.

"Yeah, exactly. The guy who had Bobby Mo's job back then, Miles Akley, got caught trying to buy a player for Louisiana. He got fired, and they hired Bobby Mo. He's a sleazebag, too, but not like Akley was. And he's actually not as bad as some of the other guys."

They walked past a row of open-air portrait painters, fortune-tellers, and NCAA-official-merchandise vendors all setting up for the day. They got a table at the café, and after they'd ordered café au lait and beignets, Chip said, "Okay, Susan Carol. You have Wojenski's number there?"

She gave it to him and he dialed it on the cell. "Dean Wojenski?" he said. "Chip Graber. I hope you're up."

He listened for a moment. "No, it's really me. Thanks. I was lucky. But I'm kind of in a jam now, like my sister told you yesterday. She said you thought you could help?" He listened for a while, then nodded and looked at Susan Carol. "Yes, she got the directions." Susan Carol nodded in confirmation. "We have to pick up a car. I think we can be there between nine-thirty and ten, if that's okay for you."

He nodded again. "Great. We'll see you in a little while."

He snapped the phone closed. "He'll be waiting for us," he said.

"Did he find a copy of your transcript?" Stevie asked.

"No, not yet. He said he'd keep looking—that it might be buried in his computer somewhere. God, wouldn't it be amazing if he had it?"

They were all quiet, thinking how much was riding on one year-old computer file.

"Won't anyone miss you, Chip?" Susan Carol said as they ate. "Where do you have to be today?"

"Press conference is at one," Graber said. "We practice at four. I've got some time."

About twenty minutes later, a green Jeep SUV pulled up in front of the café, and a tall, middle-aged man with short black hair and an equally black goatee jumped out. He was dressed in a lime green sweat suit that said BRICKLEY on it. He walked over to Graber without so much as a glance at Stevie and Susan Carol.

"Grabes!" he said, hugging Chip like a long-lost brother. "What a performance last night! You made yourself some serious bucks, kid."

It had never occurred to Stevie to think of Graber's 38 points and last-second heroics in terms of money. Which, he quickly decided, was naive.

"Thanks, man," Graber said, untangling himself from Bobby Mo. "I want you to meet my cousins—Stevie and Susan Carol."

"Nice to meet you, kids," Bobby Mo said, offering Stevie

one of those silly soul handshakes that had gone out about twenty years ago. He took Susan Carol's hand in both of his, smiled at her, and said, "Aren't you pretty?"

"Nice to meet you, too," Susan Carol said, clearly wanting to get as far away from him as possible.

Bobby Mo turned to Graber. "Brought your wheels, man. Can you drop me off back downtown?"

"No can do, pal," Graber said. "We aren't going back that way. I'm really sorry."

"No problem at all!" Bobby Mo enthused. "I'll just catch a cab. You go have a good time."

He and Graber exchanged a soul shake and another hug. "Thanks, man," Chip said. "I really appreciate you doing this."

"Just remember who has your back, okay?" Bobby Mo said.

"Always," Chip said.

He walked around to the driver's side.

"Front or back?" Stevie said to Susan Carol.

"Your call," she said.

"I'll take the back," he said. "You have the directions."

They all climbed in, waved to Bobby Mo, and Graber pulled out. "Chip, you know we have to go back through downtown to follow these directions, don't you?" Susan Carol said.

"Yeah, I know," Graber said. "But I didn't want to have to make conversation with him. You spend too much time around those guys, you start to feel the slime washing all over you."

"Will you sign with them?" Susan Carol asked.

"I have no idea. I'm going to wait until the draft. If I go as high as these agents say I'm going to go, I'll be in a position to get a lot of money."

"Do you think you'll go number one?" Stevie asked.

"No. No one is going to draft a five-foot-eleven guard with the number one pick. Too risky. They'll go for a six-eleven high school kid first. But I'm told I'll go in the top five. The Celtics look like they're going to be drafting high, and I read a quote someplace where Red Auerbach said I was the next Tiny Archibald."

Stevie had no idea who Tiny Archibald was. He assumed by the name that he was a little guard. He *did* know who Red Auerbach was, because his dad ranted constantly about all the championships Auerbach and the Celtics had stolen from the 76ers.

Chip sighed. "It's all such a crapshoot. Sometimes I think I should just sign my contract when the time comes and not bother with all this other stuff. But there's *so* much money on the table potentially."

"All of which would go down the drain if you don't throw the national championship game," Stevie said, then was sorry he had.

"Or if I get caught throwing it," Graber said darkly.

"Which is why we have to stop these guys from blackmailing you," Susan Carol said.

A road sign loomed on the right, directing them to I-10 East. "This is it," Chip said, pulling into the exit lane. "Next stop, Bay St. Louis."

14: DEAN WOJENSKI

THE TRIP TOOK JUST UNDER AN HOUR. Because the MapQuest directions were so precise, they had no trouble winding their way to the little road where Dean Wojenski lived. The house was directly across the street from the beach, and even at nine-thirty in the morning, a pretty stiff breeze was coming in off the water.

"What body of water is that?" Susan Carol said as they got out of the car.

"The Gulf of Mexico?" Chip guessed.

If he was wrong, Stevie certainly wasn't in a position to argue. Benjamin Wojenski was standing on his front porch to greet them. He looked exactly the way Stevie would expect a retired college professor and dean to look: distinguished, white hair, medium height and build.

Stevie guessed he was in his seventies, although he was clearly in good shape. Even on a cool, windy morning he was wearing shorts, moccasin shoes with no socks, and a golf shirt.

"Not often we get a true celebrity visiting here in Bay St. Louis," the old dean said, smiling broadly.

"Being a celebrity is overrated," Chip said, shaking his extended hand. "I've found that out in a hurry."

The dean laughed. "And who have we here?" he said.

They had talked about this in the car to get their stories straight.

"Well, you've talked to my sister," Chip said, pointing at Susan Carol. "This is my cousin, Stevie Thomas."

The dean shook both their hands. Then he looked at Chip. "You say you're in trouble, Chip, and I'm happy to help. But let's drop the charade. You don't have a sister and I'm guessing this isn't your cousin."

Stevie glanced at Chip to see his reaction to being caught in a solid lie. The dean had folded his arms, waiting for an answer. Stevie wondered if Susan Carol might jump in with one of her quick-thinking explanations, but she was also looking at Chip. This one was up to him.

"How'd you know?" he asked.

The dean laughed. "What do you think, Chip, that everyone in academics spends his life living under a rock? I've been following your career for years. Plus, your dad and I know each other from way back. So let's start over. Why don't you introduce me to your friends."

Chip didn't argue. He reintroduced Stevie and Susan

Carol and told the dean who they were and then added, "They're trying to help me."

"Come sit down," the dean said. "And tell me what's going on."

He led them to a screened porch that faced the water. "Great view," Chip said.

"Yes. My wife and I thought about retiring in Rhode Island, where we're both from, but after all those Minnesota winters we thought we deserved a little time in the sun."

Once they were all seated on the porch, they got down to business. Chip began with his story about Professor Whiting, and Susan Carol took over to explain how they had accidentally gotten involved. When they were finished, the dean was gaping at them.

"You said there was a problem, but this is much worse than I imagined. This is really serious. What are you going to do?" he asked. "Are you prepared to have Whiting and whoever else is involved release those transcripts if you don't throw the game tomorrow night?"

"Well, that's where you come in. Did you find my transcript on your computer? That would prove they changed the grade."

"No, I'm so sorry. I don't have it here. I thought I might, but it's gone."

"But do you remember? If you back me on the fact that I only failed the one class last spring, their whole scheme comes tumbling down."

The dean sat back on the couch. "Maybe," he said. "I mean, yes, of course I remember. I checked all athletes' transcripts carefully to be sure they were eligible. If you weren't, I would have known. But there's still the F that Whiting gave you in the fall. Even without two F's in the spring, that one would make you ineligible right now."

"But if we can prove they're lying about one transcript, people would have to think they're lying about the other one," Stevie said.

"Good point, Steve," the dean said. "But you haven't *got* proof. You've got the word of the player in question and the memory of a retired old man. And they have a physical transcript. Whom would you believe?"

Chip buried his head in his hands and groaned.

Susan Carol jumped in. "How do they *have* this transcript? Who could have changed the grade?"

"Well, Whiting could change the one from last semester easily. Professors change grades all the time—usually from an Incomplete to a letter grade, or they grade someone up because they complete a paper or retake a test for some reason. But still, a professor changing a B to an F should have raised a red flag."

"Like with Dean Mattie?" Chip asked.

"Who's he?" Stevie said.

"My replacement," Dean Wojenski said. "Theoretically, yes. Although I have to admit I might have missed a mid-semester change. And there's no reason to be looking for a grade change in March that *hurts* a student. *That* just doesn't happen."

"But what about my Econ grade?" Chip said. "We *know* Professor Scott didn't change my grade."

Dean Wojenski shook his head. "No, he didn't, poor fellow," he said. "And, unless he's some kind of computer genius, Tom Whiting didn't either. He must have had help."

"But from who?" Stevie asked.

"*Whom,*" the old professor corrected. "That's the question. Department heads can change grades. That'd be Ron Ratto in Econ. Or someone higher up in the school hierarchy. Deans, the provost, the president . . ."

"That leaves a lot of candidates, doesn't it?" Chip said.

"I'm afraid it does, Chip," Dean Wojenski said. "And some formidable ones. I'm starting to really worry for you here, Chip. There must be a lot at stake for these people. Trying to fix a game is a federal crime."

"Really?"

"Oh, yes. Legal betting takes place across state lines, so gaming and gambling are policed by the FBI. Chip, I'm worried you might be in serious danger. And maybe your friends here, too. You don't want to mess with these people."

"I don't know what to think," said Chip. "I'm so confused."

"I'm sorry—you came to me for help and I've been anything but helpful."

They all sat back in silence, feeling defeated.

"I've been wondering," Wojenski said, "how did you track me down? I got a message from someone at Davidson that you were looking for me, but before I could call back, I heard from you, Susan Carol."

"It wasn't easy. No one at MSU would help me," Chip said. "Everyone claimed to not know where you were or that they couldn't help me find you because you were entitled to your privacy in retirement. It was really weird because, to be honest, most of the time I get whatever I want around that place."

"That *is* strange. But if there are higher-ups at MSU involved, I guess it makes sense."

"Yeah, but luckily I remembered you used to be at Davidson, so I tried the alumni office."

"Well, aren't you resourceful. And someone there helped you out?"

"Yes, Christine Braman," Susan Carol said. "I thought you had talked to her. Didn't you give her the okay for us to call you?"

"No," the dean said. "I mean, I was about to, but then I heard from you directly. What was her name again?"

"Christine Braman," Susan Carol said.

The old dean sat back in his chair, clearly puzzled and disturbed. "I think we may have just found a key clue," he said. "But it would make the story even murkier. Let me get some coffee and think for a minute—can I get you some?"

They all said no, and he probably wasn't gone for more than a few minutes, but Stevie was squirming with anticipation by the time he returned. So were Chip and Susan Carol.

"Well, I'm not sure what to make of it, but that name does have something to do with you, so maybe there's a connection," Dean Wojenski said as he sat back down. "Chip, you're too young to remember this, but when Coach Pritchett left Davidson to take the job at Northern

Wisconsin, your dad was the number two assistant."

"Number two?" Chip said. "I didn't know that. I always thought he was number one. . . ."

"Because he was made the head coach, right? What happened was that Terry Hanson, who was the athletic director back then, leapfrogged your dad to make him the head coach because he thought your dad was, well, a better person than the number one guy. There were some questions about the number one guy, and a school like Davidson probably didn't want to take a chance on him getting into trouble. Squeaky-clean image and all that."

"So who was the number one guy?" Chip asked.

"Steve Jurgensen."

"I've heard that name," Chip said. "From my dad, I guess."

"Really? Do you know anything about him?"

Chip shook his head. "No."

"Well, his wife's name is Christine. She works in the alumni office at Davidson, and her maiden name was—"

"Braman," Susan Carol broke in.

"And she probably still uses that name at work," Chip said. "Which explains why I couldn't find her in the phone book."

Dean Wojenski continued, his audience now paying rapt attention. "Steve Jurgensen was angry, bitter that he didn't get hired. He told people your dad had put the knife in his back to get the job, which, from everything I knew, could not have been further from the truth."

"My dad's not like that," Chip said.

"I know, Chip. Anyway, Steve Jurgensen decided coaching wasn't for him at that point, and as it turned out, they did him a favor. He'd gotten a law degree from North Carolina while he was a young coach, so he got a job in a Charlotte law firm and within ten years had become one of the managing partners. He started to give a lot of money to his alma mater, and, I don't know, four or five years ago, they made him a member of the board of trustees. If I'm not wrong, he's on the executive committee now, and on track to be chairman of the board in a few years."

"What's his alma mater?" Susan Carol asked.

The dean smiled. "Duke."

"Duke!" they all shouted in unison, looking at one another.

"I don't remember a player named Steve Jurgensen," Susan Carol said. "And I know most of the Duke players going back to the 1960s."

"He wasn't a player," Professor Wojenski said. "He was a manager."

"A manager who became a coach?" Chip asked.

"That's not unusual," Stevie said. "Lawrence Frank of the New Jersey Nets was a manager at Indiana."

"And Jeff LaMere at Virginia Commonwealth was a manager for Coach K," Susan Carol added.

"The difference is, he left coaching and got rich," the dean said.

Stevie could see Chip doing the same kind of mental two-plus-two that he was doing. "Okay, let's just say this Steve Jurgensen is involved in this somehow," Chip said.

"He's still carrying a grudge against my father and he wants to see him lose and Duke win. How does he hook up with Whiting?"

"It *would* help explain why Whiting made the comment about playing Duke in the final," Stevie said to Chip. "Maybe it wouldn't have mattered to Jurgensen if you guys were playing UConn."

"Maybe not," Chip said. "But if Jurgensen and Whiting are in this together, why would Jurgensen's wife help us find you, Dean?"

"Yes, why?" the dean said. "Maybe he knew I'd be unlikely to be much help and hoped you'd be discouraged. Maybe he thought you were on to something and he wanted to divert suspicion from himself by seeming to help you."

"But we can't be sure that Jurgensen is involved at all, can we?" Susan Carol asked.

"If he's not, it's one hell of a coincidence," Dean Wojenski said.

"I don't believe anything is coincidence at this point," Chip said.

Chip stood up and looked at his watch. "I have to get back downtown for a press conference," he said. "Thanks for seeing us, Dean Wojenski. You've been a big help."

"Not really, I'm afraid. What will you do, Chip?"

"I'm handing it over to these two."

"Us?" Stevie said.

"You bet. My guess is Steve Jurgensen is in New Orleans to watch his alma mater win the national championship tomorrow night. You guys have got to find him."

■ ■ ■

Once they were back in the car and headed back to New Orleans, Chip gave Susan Carol his cell phone so she could try to call Bill Brill. They knew the Duke team wasn't staying at its assigned hotel downtown, but Brill had said the rooms were being used by alumni, fans, and donors. Problem was, neither of them could remember the name of the hotel. Brill would know.

They got lucky. Susan Carol caught him walking out the door to get a late breakfast before the press conferences. It was getting close to noon and Chip was pushing eighty as he pulled onto I-10. Susan Carol talked to Brill briefly, said she wasn't sure she would be at the press conferences—which were being held at the Dome—and then closed the phone.

"He says the Duke players are out by the airport; the fans and alums are at the Embassy Suites, but the really big shots are at the Windsor Court," she said. "He even had the phone number because he's been trying to call the chairman of the board for a story he's writing on their search for a new president."

"Well, if the chairman is staying there . . . ," Stevie said.

"Right." She dialed the number and asked for Steve Jurgensen. A moment later, she hung up. "She said she would ring the room. I hung up when it started to ring."

"Okay then," Chip said. "We know where the guy is. Now—" He stopped himself and glanced in the rearview mirror.

"What is it?" Susan Carol asked.

"Company," Chip said. "I think someone's following us." Stevie started to turn around but heard Chip say, "Don't look back."

"Are you sure?" Susan Carol asked.

"No. Could be a coincidence, but that black Town Car got on the highway at the same place we did, and he's been staying the same distance behind us ever since."

"So what do you want to do?" Stevie asked.

"I want to find out if I'm paranoid or not," he said, suddenly swerving the car to the right onto an exit ramp. He pulled up the ramp, glancing in the mirror as he did. At the top of the ramp, he grimaced. "Our friend got off, too," he said.

Stevie felt a slight tremor go through him. "Maybe we should get right back on the highway," he said.

"Easy, Stevie," Chip said. "Look, there are gas stations and fast-food places right here. I think we could use some gas."

He swung the car into an Exxon station on the right. As they pulled up to the pumps, they saw the Town Car go past them.

"Hey," Stevie said, "maybe . . . oh."

"No, they're following us, all right," Chip said as they all watched the car make a quick left into the Burger King diagonally across the street from the Exxon. "They're just going to wait for us over there."

"What should we do?" Stevie asked.

"Get some gas and get back to town," Chip said.

He hopped out of the car and began pumping gas while

Susan Carol and Stevie kept an eye on the car. It had pulled around to the section of the Burger King parking lot that faced the gas station.

"No one's getting out," Susan Carol said. "They're just sitting there waiting for us to leave."

"Well, who is it? Why are they following us?" Stevie asked.

"I could maybe find out who . . . ," Susan Carol said as Chip got back in the car. "Chip, go to the drive-thru at that Burger King."

"You're *hungry*?" Chip asked.

"No, but from the drive-thru window we'll have a perfect view of his license plate. I have a friend who might be able to trace it."

They got lucky because there was no line. Chip ordered a hamburger, three fries, and three Cokes. When they pulled up to the window, Susan Carol and Stevie squinted at the back of the car while Chip paid. The windows were tinted, so they couldn't see inside. Never had a car seemed so ominous.

"Oh my God," Susan Carol said. "It's a North Carolina plate!"

"Can you make it out?" Chip said, pulling a bag of food into the car and passing it to the backseat without looking back.

"I can," said Stevie, always proud of his vision. "DTC-145."

"Someone write that down," Chip said, accepting his change, "and let's get out of here."

Stevie didn't need to write it down—he wasn't likely to forget it—but Susan Carol whipped out her notebook.

Chip pulled out quickly and they were back on the interstate in under a minute. Soon after, Chip glanced in the mirror and said, "They're right back with us."

Susan Carol called her friend and gave him the plate number.

"Who *was* that?" Stevie was incredulous. "You really know someone who can track down a license plate?"

"He's a friend. His father's a big shot in the state police and he can get into his computer. Once his dad caught him checking out the license plates of all the teachers at school to find out if any of them had ever been in trouble."

"But he's still willing to do this for you?" Stevie asked.

"Oh, yeah."

"And he didn't ask *why* you need to know this?"

She blushed. "He kind of likes me. He said he'd call back as soon as he could."

That answer didn't exactly thrill Stevie, but he resisted the urge to ask more questions.

Chip looked at his watch. It was almost twelve-thirty. He asked Susan Carol for his cell phone back and dialed a number. "Tom, it's Grabes," he said. "Do me a favor, tell my dad and Coach Ames I'm not going over to the Dome with the team, that I'll meet them there. I might be a minute or two late but don't panic. I just had to do something."

He snapped the phone shut.

"Okay, what now?" he said. "We know where Jurgensen is staying, but how does that help us?"

"Should we try to find him at his hotel? Talk to him?" Stevie asked.

"Or maybe just follow him?" Susan Carol offered. "See where he goes and who he talks to?"

"He could talk to lots of people, but how will we know who they are?" said Stevie, feeling frustrated.

"True," Susan Carol admitted. "We don't even know what *he* looks like. . . ."

Chip's cell phone broke into their conversation. It was Susan Carol's friend, calling back with a name to go with the license-plate number.

"Well, we don't have to wonder how to find Steve Jurgensen anymore," she said, hanging up. "He's right behind us."

"What?!" Stevie and Chip yelled in near-perfect unison.

The idea of following Jurgensen was decidedly less creepy than the reality of being followed *by* him.

"Yeah," said Susan Carol shakily, "how's *that* for a coincidence?"

"I knew he had to be connected . . . ," said Chip, slamming his palm on the steering wheel. "Damn it. I wonder if he followed us *out* there, too? That means he's seen you guys. And if you went to see Wojenski with me, then he'll know you *know*. . . ."

"Oh, great," said Stevie, almost too scared to even process what that might mean.

"Okay, don't panic. These guys are more interested in me than in you," said Chip. "If you guys come to the Dome with me, I'll bet you can lose him there. You have press clearance and Jurgensen doesn't. You have your credentials on you?"

For once, Stevie was prepared. "I stuck it in the back of my notebook just in case," he said. "Susan Carol?"

"Got it."

"Okay," Chip said. "Once we're in, you guys can take off and probably not be followed."

"Probably not?" Stevie said.

"Stevie, no guarantees right now," Chip said. "You want out?"

"No! That's not what I meant."

"Okay, then," he said. "Who's got an idea?"

"I do," Susan Carol said.

"Of course you do," Stevie said.

Chip laughed. "Okay, little sister," he said. "Let's hear it."

He picked up his speed a little more, and they flew along the highway, the black Town Car keeping pace not far behind.

15: FINDING PROOF

IT WAS ONE O'CLOCK precisely when Chip wheeled the car up to the gate behind the Superdome that was marked NCAA PERSONNEL ONLY. The Town Car was holding a block back. He rolled down the window as a guard walked up to greet them, waving his hand to indicate they were in the wrong place.

"Chip Graber—Minnesota State," Chip said to the guard, showing him his player pin and his driver's license. "I'm due inside for the press conference right now."

"Sorry, pal, no one parks in here without a pass," he said. "The van with the Minnesota State people just came through here a couple minutes ago."

"I know," Chip said. "I had to run an errand with my

cousins here, so I missed the team van. I was told to meet everyone here."

The guard was still shaking his head when a second guard walked over to see what the problem was. The first one hooked a thumb at Chip and said, "Kid claims he's a player. He's got a pin but no parking pass."

"Player, yeah right," the second guard said. He bent down a little to look in the open window, and Stevie saw his eyes go wide. "Chip Graber? Holy . . ." He stopped before the next word came out of his mouth. "Bill, it's Chip Graber. Open the damn gate, will ya? Chip, sorry, thought you'd come with the other guys. No one told us. . . ."

"It's okay," Chip said, waving his hand as if granting forgiveness.

"Go right in there and up to the ramp," the second guard said. "There's spots down there. You know how to get to the interview room from there, right? There's signs and all. . . ."

"Yeah, yeah. Got it," Chip said. "Thanks."

The gate opened and he pulled through with a wave to Bill, and they watched the black Town Car continue slowly down the block.

Chip got almost to the entrance of the building before parking. It had started to rain again and they walked quickly to the nearby door. The guard there was insistent that Stevie and Susan Carol go outside, upstairs, and over the ramp to the media entrance. He said that he knew who Chip was and that he was expected at the press conference but orders were orders.

"Get someone from the NCAA out here," Chip said.

"What?"

"You've got a walkie-talkie right there. Call someone."

"Look, you can go in," the guard said. "You're fine. They just have to go up and around."

"I understand," Chip said. "But I'm not going inside without these guys."

The guard rolled his eyes and picked up his walkie-talkie. "NCAA public relations, come in please," he said.

A voice crackled back. "PR here, what's up?"

"I've got a student-athlete at the back door."

"Graber? Chip Graber, I hope."

"Yeah and—"

"Well, send him in, for crying out loud. He's late."

"He's got two kids here with press credentials. I told him they had to go around to the media entrance."

"Right."

"He won't come in without them."

Stevie heard a profanity come through the walkie-talkie. No more than sixty seconds later, a blue-blazered man with what looked like a very bad toupee rounded the corner with an exasperated look on his face.

He pointed his walkie-talkie at Graber. "Come on, Chip, you're late. Let's go."

Chip pointed at Susan Carol and Stevie. "They have credentials. Let them in, too."

The blazer shook his head. "Can't make exceptions. They have to go around."

For the first time since he had met Chip Graber, Stevie

saw him really get angry. He walked right up to the blazer and pointed a finger at his chest.

"Listen, jerk, I'm tired of all this NCAA crap. All the rules, and the student-athlete mumbo jumbo, and no exceptions. I've been hearing it for three weeks in three cities. Here's the deal: You take all three of us back there *now* or we all leave *now*. And then you can go in there and explain to the national media that I'm not at the press conference the day before the championship game because *you* couldn't do anything except recite the freaking rules."

The bad toupee was clearly surprised that a student-athlete would speak to him this way. He backed up from Chip to clear some space. "Look, Chip, let's talk about this later. . . ."

"*Now,*" Chip said. "Five seconds and I walk."

The guy looked at Chip as if trying to decide if he was bluffing. Apparently he decided he wasn't. "Okay, okay. Come on. But your school will be penalized for you being late, and I will report this to the basketball committee."

"Yeah, go right ahead," Chip said. "Maybe they'll declare me ineligible to play tomorrow, huh? Your friends at CBS would love that."

The blazer wheeled and began talking into his walkie-talkie again. "Bringing Graber now," he said.

As soon as they reached the interview room, the blazer pointed Chip to the back entrance that would lead to the podium. Stevie could hear Coach Graber talking over the microphone about how much respect he had for Duke and Coach Krzyzewski.

"Okay," Stevie said to Susan Carol, "I'll go find Brill while you call our dads to tell them we came straight to the press conference. I'll meet you in the press room in a few minutes."

She nodded and headed off. Stevie walked into the back of the interview room and scanned for Bill Brill. Fortunately, he wasn't sitting down; he was standing off to the side in a purple-and-green sweater, arms folded, not taking notes. Stevie walked over and lightly tugged on his arm.

"Hey," Brill whispered. "You guys okay? Where's Susan Carol?"

"She's in the press room making a call. Can I talk to you outside for a minute?"

Brill shrugged. "Sure," he said. "I don't need to listen to this."

Once they were outside the room, Stevie came right to the point. "Susan Carol said you were trying to reach the chairman of Duke's board of trustees to set up an interview, is that right?"

"Right," Brill said, looking a bit baffled at Stevie's sudden interest in Duke. "*Blue Devil Weekly* has a special edition coming out on Wednesday on the Final Four and the search for a new president, so I'm doing a story."

"Why does the new president matter to a magazine that's about sports?" Stevie said, getting a little sidetracked, but curious.

"The president of a college affects athletics a lot," Brill said. "If Duke gets someone like the woman before Sanford, who didn't get sports at all, Krzyzewski won't be happy. And they need him happy, because he's the school's most important fund-raiser. And there are questions about what they're going to do about football. . . ."

"Football?"

"Yes, believe it or not, there are some people who still care about football."

"They play football at Duke?"

"Badly. Very badly."

"Okay, okay." Stevie realized he was way off topic and Brill was starting to look at him just a little bit suspiciously. "So, who's the board chairman?"

"Stuart M. Feeley, software billionaire. Sort of the East Coast's answer to Bill Gates. Knows not a damn thing about basketball, but I have been granted an audience at four-thirty this afternoon."

That was exactly what Stevie was hoping to hear. "Could you take Susan Carol and me with you?" he said. "We don't want a story, we just want to watch you conduct the interview. We both think we would learn a lot."

"Well . . . ," Brill said, hesitating. "I guess that's fine. But where is she again? Why isn't she asking me about this, too?"

"She's in the press room talking to her dad. He's a little upset with her because we kind of wandered off together this morning and forgot to call."

Brill smiled. "Oh, okay." He patted Stevie on the back. "Good for you."

Stevie tried to give him what he thought might be a conspiratorial look. He had no idea if he succeeded.

"I'll meet you here as soon as Duke is finished," Brill said.

Stevie shook his head. "Actually, can we just meet you in the hotel lobby? We both need to write our stories for today and our computers are back at the Hyatt.

"We went to an FCA prayer breakfast and talked to some people," Stevie went on. "But we both admitted that interviewing people was hard—that's why we thought we'd like to see how you do it."

"Well, that was good thinking by both of you to go to the breakfast instead of writing this press-conference garbage. Fine then, meet me in the lobby of the Windsor Court Hotel at a little bit before four-thirty. Do you think you can find it okay?"

"Oh yeah, we have a good map. Thanks, Mr. Brill."

Brill turned to go back inside the interview room. Stevie went in the other direction, circling the arena to the media workroom. It was virtually empty and Susan Carol was just hanging up the phone when Stevie arrived.

"Did you get our dads?" he said.

"Just yours. My dad wasn't in his room, so I left him a long message. Your dad stayed in to watch golf because the weather's so lousy. I told him we had run long this morning, then came over here to listen to the press conferences. I told him we would be back a little before dinnertime. He said that my dad was going to call him soon to see if he had heard from us. So, they should be fine."

"At least for a few hours."

■ ■ ■

They walked briskly back to the hotel through the rain. Susan Carol went to her room to pick up her computer while Stevie picked up sandwiches and sodas for them in the lobby café, and then they met in the Hyatt's press room to get to work.

They had three hours to concoct some sort of story for their papers and do as much background research on both Steve Jurgensen and Stuart Feeley as possible.

Earlier, when they were in the car with Chip, they had decided that someone else had to be brought into the circle, someone with authority. Susan Carol had lobbied hard for calling the FBI, but Chip wasn't ready for that yet. Stevie thought they should try Bobby Kelleher, since he'd uncovered that Brickley Shoe scandal, but a reporter sounded even worse to Chip. Finally they settled on a Duke official—the chairman of the board of trustees, Stuart M. Feeley.

They would tell him about Steve Jurgensen and the plot against Chip Graber and his dad. Then they would ask Feeley to confront Jurgensen and tell him to back off or face immediate banishment from the board and, potentially, criminal charges. No harm, no foul, Chip called it. If he agreed to stop blackmailing Chip and told Whiting it was all over, they wouldn't call the authorities. They were hoping that Feeley would be just as eager to avoid the scandal of a Duke trustee trying to fix a game as they were.

"I don't see how Jurgensen can do anything except back down," Stevie said when they had discussed the plan.

"Unless he's already made a big bet," said Susan Carol.

"Lose a bet or go to jail. Which would you choose?"

"We can only hope."

Susan Carol started writing a piece about Final Four fever in the Big Easy that they'd file under both their names. It was the best they could come up with on short notice.

Stevie's computer search didn't reveal much more than they already knew, except that Feeley did not have an especially warm relationship with Duke president Tom Sanford. There was some speculation that Sanford's decision to retire at age fifty-eight had as much to do with Feeley as with wanting to do less fund-raising. Good to know, Stevie guessed.

He searched through the Duke media guide, but the bios of Sanford and Feeley were glowing and unhelpful. And Jurgensen didn't even rate a bio, just a listing as a trustee. No picture, no nothing.

When Susan Carol was finished, Stevie began editing the story to add his perspective. The piece was full of color and amusing anecdotes. He had to admit, she was a good writer.

"Nice piece of fiction, Scarlett," he said.

"Thanks," Susan Carol replied. "It's the weekend I was expecting to have."

"What are you writing now?" Stevie asked as she was still typing rapid-fire.

"I'm writing up some notes on everything that's *really* happened so far. I just think it would be good to have a backup copy."

"Yeah, and you'd like to send it to the FBI, too, wouldn't you?"

"Not yet. But maybe."

They left the hotel shortly before four o'clock. The Windsor Court Hotel was conveniently close to the Hilton, so they hopped on the hotel shuttle again. It was a really fancy hotel, its lobby filled with oriental carpets, oil paintings, and flowers. They sat on a velvet settee by the door to keep an eye out for Brill and felt massively underdressed.

Almost as soon as they sat down, two men walked past, heading for the street. One of their voices snapped Stevie to attention. "It's still a slam dunk" was all he heard. He knew that voice. He looked up just in time to see Thomas R. Whiting, dressed, Stevie was convinced, in the same charcoal gray suit he had been wearing Friday, holding the door for another man. He wondered if it was Jurgensen.

Stevie quickly followed them to the door, hoping he could casually walk outside and somehow get ahead of them so he could get a better look at the second man's face. No such luck. A car was waiting for them, and Whiting and his companion slid inside before Stevie could even get through the door. Dammit, Stevie thought. He explained what he'd heard to Susan Carol, who had an idea. She found a house phone and asked for Steve Jurgensen's room. She was prepared to hang up if someone answered, but there was no need. On the fourth ring the phone flipped over to voice mail asking her to leave a message.

That didn't exactly confirm that it was Jurgensen with Whiting, but it was possible.

"Well," Susan Carol said, "Whiting's got one thing right:

this is going to be a slam dunk. But not the one he had in mind."

■ ■ ■

Brill walked into the lobby looking a little bit exasperated at four-thirty on the dot. "Couldn't get a cab," he said. "Feeley's not the kind of guy you want to be late for. Let's go."

"Did you tell him you were bringing us?"

"I left a message for his assistant so it wouldn't be a complete surprise. I told him to call me back if there was a problem, and I didn't get any messages on my cell."

They crossed the lobby to the elevators. Since there were no players and coaches staying in the hotel, there was no security. Brill punched in a code on the keypad above the floor numbers when they got in. "He's in some kind of penthouse suite," he said. "They gave me the code to get up there."

The elevator took them to the twenty-second floor in a matter of seconds. When they got off, they *were* greeted by a security guard.

"Mr. Brill?"

"Yes," Brill said.

"Mr. Feeley's expecting you. Follow me."

He led them down the hallway but they could hardly get lost—there appeared to be only one room on the floor. He knocked softly on the door and it was answered almost immediately by a tall hulk of a man who was dressed in a silly-looking flowered shirt and khaki pants.

"Mr. Brill," the security man said when the door opened, "and friends."

The hulk pulled the door open and gave Brill a quizzical look.

"I left you a message, Gary," Brill said as they walked into the wide entryway of the suite. "These are the two winners of the USBWA writing contest. They're here for the weekend to observe journalists working at the Final Four, and they wanted to sit in on my interview with Mr. Feeley."

The guy in the flowered shirt didn't even look at Stevie or Susan Carol. "That will be up to Mr. Feeley," he said, and led the way through the entryway to a spectacularly large room that had a panoramic view of the waterfront. The room was twice as big as the one Chip Graber had and a lot fancier.

Stuart M. Feeley had been sitting in a big armchair near the window, watching the golf tournament on the largest-screen TV Stevie had ever seen. As soon as he heard people come into the room, he stood up and turned to greet his guests. He had a cigar in one hand and wore a blue golf shirt that said DUKE BASKETBALL on it, shorts, and no shoes. If he was upset to see that Brill had company, he didn't show it.

Before Flower Shirt could say anything, Feeley crossed the room with his hand out. "Bill, good to see you again," he said. "I see you've brought company. Grandkids? Friends? Assistants?"

"None of the above," Brill said. "Well, friends, yes." He introduced Stevie and Susan Carol and again explained who they were and why they were here.

"Well, I'm flattered that you would think I had anything

interesting to say," Feeley said. "You kids want something to drink? Bill?"

Brill asked for a beer and Stevie and Susan Carol each asked for a Coke. Gary, clearly dismayed, went off to find the drinks, and Feeley offered them all chairs near the window, while he picked up a remote and turned off the TV.

"Who's leading?" Brill asked.

"A guy named Paul Goydos," Feeley said. "Ever heard of him?"

"Yeah. I read about him in a book about the tour years ago. I didn't even know he was still playing."

"Well, he's two shots ahead of Davis Love and Billy Andrade, with three holes to play."

Stevie liked Stuart Feeley almost immediately. He was obviously a very wealthy man but didn't act as if that somehow made him important. If his assistant was put off by Stevie and Susan Carol's presence, *he* clearly wasn't bothered by it at all. He asked them each questions about their backgrounds while they waited for the drinks.

"So, Susan Carol's bringing you around on Coach K and Duke," he said when Stevie finished his story.

"Well," Stevie said, "maybe just a little."

Once they had been served their drinks, Brill started asking questions about how the search for a new president was going—what Feeley was looking for, and if there was any truth to the rumors that Sanford was retiring because of disagreements with Feeley. If that question troubled Feeley, he didn't show it. "Bill, I'm not going to sit here and tell you that Tom and I never disagreed," he said. "We did. But as far as I was concerned, he could be president of Duke for life. He's a brilliant guy who did great things for the school. This was strictly his decision."

Stevie couldn't help but think that he had answered a question that hadn't been asked. Brill hadn't asked if he had forced Sanford to retire, only if their relationship was behind his retiring. Brill kept a tape recorder running during the interview, and Susan Carol took notes to make it look as if they were really interested. Susan Carol may have been. By the time Brill started asking about possible candidates—a question Feeley clearly wasn't going to touch—Stevie was almost bored, a first for the weekend.

And then a couple of minutes later it was over. Everyone was standing up and shaking hands. This was Susan Carol's cue.

"Mr. Feeley, I don't want to impose"—Stevie noticed she had the full Southern accent working: *aah doan want ta immmpose*—"but could you give me just another minute or two on an entirely different topic that I'm hoping to write something about?"

"Well," Feeley said, looking at his watch, "I have a cocktail party to go to before dinner. . . ."

"It really won't take very long."

Feeley smiled. "Sure, absolutely."

Now it was Stevie's turn. "Come on, Mr. Brill, let's wait in the lobby," he said.

Brill was clearly a bit confused but unbothered by Susan Carol's sudden boldness. "Susan Carol, don't be long, I need to get back to the hotel and write."

They left Susan Carol alone with Feeley. Stevie and Susan Carol had decided it was better for her to talk to him one-on-one rather than gang up.

"So, what in the world is that about?" Brill said after the security guard had led them back to the elevator.

Stevie rolled his eyes. "She writes for some newsletter at her dad's church. She wanted to ask him about religion and sports and the role the two of them play in college life."

Brill smiled at him as the elevator rocketed downward. "Religion make you uncomfortable?" he asked.

"No, not at all," Stevie said. "I'm just amazed by how much of it there is here. I mean, what's the connection between God and sports?"

"I think it's partly insecurity," Brill said. "Success in sports is so fleeting. And so tenuous. A lot of guys are looking for something to hang on to."

That made sense to Stevie. They had reached the lobby. Brill looked at his watch.

"If you need to get going, Mr. Brill, I'll just wait here until she's done," he said.

"That would help," Brill said. "I have to write some Internet stuff before dinner. You kids can get back to the hotel okay?"

Stevie nodded. He watched Brill walk through the doors. It was almost five-thirty. Time to call his dad again even though he figured they would be going back to the hotel as soon as Susan Carol was finished with Feeley.

"You know, Reverend Anderson isn't thrilled with you

kids being gone all day like this," his dad said.

"I know, I know, we've just been real busy," Stevie said. "Would you call him and tell him Susan Carol's finishing her story and we should be back soon?"

"Okay, I'll do it," his dad said. "But no more gallivanting tonight. We should spend some time together."

"Absolutely, Dad."

Depending on how things were going upstairs, he thought, their gallivanting might soon be over.

16: CLOSING IN

IT WAS ALMOST SIX O'CLOCK by the time Susan Carol came back to the lobby. Stevie was extremely glad Brill hadn't waited around for her. A couple of times he had thought about calling the room to make sure everything was okay, but decided against it. The story she was telling would take a while. And Stuart Feeley would have a lot of questions.

For the first time all weekend, he thought she looked tired as she crossed the lobby from the elevator to where he was sitting reading the sports section of the New Orleans *Times-Picayune*.

"Everything okay?" he asked, standing up to greet her.

"I think so," she said. "Let's get back to the Hyatt before my dad has a heart attack. I'll tell you about it on the way."

Before she started her story, he told her he'd had his dad

call hers. That seemed to make her feel a little better.

"So, the good news is, I convinced him to talk to Jurgensen," she said as a clap of thunder overhead reminded them that it was about to rain again.

"Is there bad news?"

"Sort of," she said. "He doesn't want us there. He thinks Jurgensen deserves the chance to explain in private."

"Explain? What's to explain?"

She held a hand up. "You're preaching to the choir, Stevie. He was very skeptical when I first started to tell him the story. I gave him Chip's cell phone number and told him he could call him to confirm. I think he finally believed me, but he thought Jurgensen would be more likely to fess up if he talked to him alone. He did say he wouldn't allow Jurgensen to stay on the board if this is true. His offer will be to not go to the FBI in return for his resignation as soon as the Final Four is over."

"When's he going to do this?"

"I don't know. They have this big deal dinner tonight for all their donors and trustees. He said it wouldn't be tonight. Probably tomorrow morning. He'll call us after he and Jurgensen talk. I think the one thing that may have convinced him is that he knew that Jurgensen had driven here for the weekend because he had business in Birmingham and decided driving was easier than flying."

"Or so he said."

"Right. We need to call Chip as soon as we get back. Their practice should be over about now."

They agreed to try to convince their dads that the four

of them should have dinner together. "I just think we should stick close," she said.

Stevie wasn't sure if that was absolutely necessary. But, he decided, it was fine with him.

■ ■ ■

Chip sounded relieved when Stevie reached him and told him about their meeting with Feeley. He was back in his room by then and said he was planning to go to sleep as soon as he'd had dinner.

Going to bed sounded pretty good to Stevie. He told Chip about their concern that Feeley had insisted on meeting privately with Jurgensen. "It's okay," Chip said. "He sounds like a pretty up-front guy. I can understand him wanting to confront Jurgensen alone."

"Well, we gave him your cell phone number just in case he wants to confirm any facts or details," Stevie said. "Susan Carol thinks he'll meet with Jurgensen in the morning. We should hear from him after that."

"We're going over to the arena for our last walk-through at about eleven o'clock," Chip said. "I'll be back in the room after that, trying to rest. Call me whenever you hear something."

"Should we come to the arena if we get word while you're over there?"

"I don't think so. You'll never get in; the walk-throughs are closed to everyone. And that NCAA guy really let my dad have it after the press conference. My dad was pretty ticked. He wanted to know what the hell I was doing running around with a couple of teenagers."

"What'd you tell him?"

Chip laughed. "I told him the truth—sort of. That you guys won the basketball writing contest and I had told you I would give you some time on Sunday before the press conferences."

"He buy it?"

"Maybe. I don't think he wants to get into any long arguments with me until this is over."

Stevie was nodding his head, forgetting that Chip couldn't see him on the other end of the phone. "We'll call you as soon as we know something," he said.

"Sounds good. Get some sleep."

"Yeah, you too."

Stevie was about to hang up when he heard Chip say, "Hey, Stevie?"

"What?"

"Thanks."

He hung up and walked back to the main lobby area to meet Susan Carol, who had come down five minutes ahead of the fathers so he could fill her in. Bill Thomas and Reverend Anderson showed up just as Stevie was finishing, and they walked two blocks to a Morton's steak house where Stevie's dad had been able to make a reservation. Dinner was quiet. Stevie's mind kept wandering to what was going to happen next. He found himself creating the meeting between Feeley and Jurgensen in his head. Susan Carol wasn't saying very much either.

"You kids are both pretty quiet," Bill Thomas said, finally.

"Just tired, Mr. Thomas," Susan Carol said. "We got up

early this morning and spent the day running around, getting quotes from people and then writing our stories."

"Being a reporter is hard work," Stevie said.

Reverend Anderson smiled. "But you are having fun, aren't you? Is it all as exciting as you hoped?"

Susan Carol and Stevie looked at each other.

"Beyond our wildest dreams," said Stevie.

■ ■ ■

Stevie was asleep almost as soon as his head hit the pillow. His body had finally run out of both energy and adrenaline. He woke up once in the middle of the night, after dreaming that Steve Jurgensen was chasing them in his big black car and they'd run out of road at the beach near Dean Wojenski's house in Bay St. Louis. He got up and drank some water, trying to shake the vision of the dream.

He woke up again at seven-thirty and found a note from his dad saying he'd gone for a walk and would be back for breakfast at eight. He had left the newspaper behind and Stevie picked through the sports section until he got to "News and Notes from the Final Four." The third item down caught his eye: "Chip Graber arrived for his team's Sunday press conference seven minutes late, explaining that he had gone sightseeing and then got stuck in traffic. NCAA media official David Kiley said MSU would be subject to a fine from the basketball committee because of Graber's lateness. 'We make no exceptions,' Kiley said. 'Rules are rules.'" Stevie could almost hear Kiley, who he assumed was the guy with the bad toupee, repeating that mantra. The next sentence was a surprise, though: "Kiley's boss, Bill Hancock, who is responsible for all working media during the NCAA tournament, was more sympathetic: 'Sometimes we forget these are still kids,' he said. 'Considering what Chip Graber has done for college basketball the last four years, and especially the last three weeks, I think we can give him seven minutes of leeway.'"

Wow, Stevie thought, an NCAA official with common sense and a heart. "He must be new or something," he said aloud, laughing as he put down the paper.

The morning passed as slowly as any Stevie could remember in his entire life. Toward the end of breakfast his father finally said to him, "Stevie, why do you keep looking at your watch every single minute?"

Stevie tried to sound as casual as he could. "It's just a big day. I need to do some pregame research and there's a lunch that Susan Carol and I have been invited to. The board of the basketball writers meets with the board of the coaches' association."

The lunch was real and Stevie and Susan Carol had been invited. And Stevie did want to go. Whether they would get to go depended on what they heard from Stuart Feeley. They were hoping he would call before noon to tell them that Jurgensen had backed down, that Whiting and friends would be called off, and that Chip could play tonight with no worries.

"Who's going to be there?" his dad asked.

"Supposedly guys like Rick Barnes from Texas and Skip Prosser from Wake Forest and Tommy Amaker from Michigan and Mike Brey from Notre Dame."

"That sounds like a good group."

"Yeah, it should be fun." Without thinking, he looked at his watch again, causing his father to laugh.

"It's one minute later than it was last time you looked," he said.

After breakfast, his dad announced that he was going to the recently opened D-Day museum. Stevie had seen signs for it around town. His dad made the mandatory father's plea that Stevie go with him, knowing it wasn't going to happen. He'd given up his visions of this as a father-son bonding weekend. "Just be sure to tell your mother I tried to get you to go," he said.

"I will, Dad."

■ ■ ■

Stevie killed time watching TV, waiting for the phone to ring. Vitale was saying that Chip Graber's performance Saturday was "the single most stupendous, spectacular, sensational performance I've seen at a Final Four since Bill Walton went 21-for-22 against Memphis State in 1973."

He was right, Stevie thought. Chip had been sensational. He hoped he would have the chance to be equally good tonight.

The phone rang—at last. He looked at the clock on the desk. It was 10:40.

"It's Chip."

"Hey, Chip," he said. "We haven't heard from Feeley yet."

"I know. I did."

"*You* did?"

"Yeah, he said you had given him my cell phone number."

Stevie had forgotten about that. "Yeah, that's right. In case he wanted to verify our story."

"Well, he didn't call to verify anything. He said he talked to Jurgensen."

"And?"

"And Jurgensen told him to go ahead and call the FBI. He said if we did that, he and Whiting would go straight to the NCAA with my transcript and I would be declared ineligible to play tonight."

"Oh God. They would do that without investigating further?"

"Oh yeah. The way the NCAA works is if they think a player is ineligible for any reason, they suspend you immediately, and then you have to apply to be reinstated."

"If you have to do that . . ."

"It'll be way too late. There would be nothing to be reinstated for."

"Well, at least we know for sure now that Jurgensen's guilty."

There was silence on the other end of the phone. "Chip, you there?"

"Yeah. I was just thinking that knowing Jurgensen is guilty doesn't do us a lot of good at the moment."

He was right—unfortunately. "What do you think we should do now?"

"I'm not sure. I have to go to shootaround right now. We'll be done at noon. I think we should meet."

"At your hotel?"

"No, the place is swarming with people. Plus, Whiting's bound to be watching me like a hawk."

"Where then?"

"Come to the arena. I'll meet you outside that media entrance they wanted you to go to. I'll be able to find it."

"What about your dad?"

"I can tell him I just need a walk by myself to clear my head. I do that sometimes on game days."

"Okay. Noon?"

"Like ten after."

"We'll be there."

He hung up. This was not the twist in the story they had been hoping for. Jurgensen had called their bluff. Chip was now back where he started: if he helped his team win the national championship, he would be the subject of a full-blown academic investigation that would land his school on probation, have his team stripped of every win this season, and potentially ruin his dad's career. Not to mention what it would do to his sneaker contract. He was pretty certain good old Bobby Mo would *not* have Chip's back if he thought he was tainted in any way. Dean Wojenski might be able to convince some people that Chip's spring transcript had been changed, but there was still Whiting's F in the fall. A tough case to win and the publicity would be brutal regardless of the outcome. But if Chip *did* throw the game, he would have to live with what he had done for the rest of his life.

Stevie called Susan Carol. She was as stunned as he had

been by the news that Jurgensen hadn't caved. "Now what do we do?" she said.

He told her that Chip wanted to meet them after his shootaround, and they agreed to meet in the lobby at eleven-thirty to walk over to the Dome.

The weather had finally turned gorgeous—the sun was out and the temperature was in the mid-seventies. If anything, the streets were more packed than they had been earlier in the week. The only difference, Stevie noticed, was that all the fans were in purple and white or blue and white. The UConn and St. Joe's contingents had, with a few exceptions, gone home.

As they made their way through the throngs, Susan Carol said quietly, "Stevie, I think we're all in over our heads here."

Stevie nodded. Things had gone so well since they started investigating that his thought until Chip's call had been "We can do this." Now that seemed almost silly.

"If we are in over our heads, what can we do now?" he said. "Who can we go to?"

She thought about that for a minute. "I guess it's up to Chip. This is his life we're talking about. But I think we need to convince him to go to the FBI or at least Bobby Kelleher."

It was 12:05 when they walked across the bridge and around the now-familiar concourse to the media entrance. There was almost no one around, so they stood and looked down to the street level, which was teeming with people. They could see several police cars and motorcycles leading the Minnesota State bus out of the parking lot and into traffic. That bus would be back in about six hours and, Steve figured, in about ten hours a national champion would be crowned. Ten hours and it would be over one way or the other. . . .

"You guys been waiting long?"

They turned and saw Chip dressed in disguise—gray sweatshirt and pants, untied sneakers, and a black cap that said US OPEN—BETHPAGE BLACK 2002.

"Chip, I'm so sorry it's turning out this way," Susan Carol said, giving him a hug.

He smiled. "Never over till it's over, right? I almost told my dad about the whole thing after I talked to Feeley this morning," he said. "But then I thought, this is supposed to be the greatest day of his career. I just couldn't put something like this on him right now."

"So instead you carry it all by yourself," Susan Carol said.

"Not exactly," Chip said. "You guys have been helping me carry it the last few days."

"Yeah, big help we've been," Stevie said. He was feeling terribly sad and helpless at that moment.

"Well, here's what I've decided to do," Chip said. "I called Feeley back and asked him for Jurgensen's cell phone number because there's no answer in the SOB's room at the hotel. I left a message but he won't call back. Feeley said he didn't have the cell number but he thought he could track him down over there. I told him I wanted to meet with him myself."

"Now?" Stevie said. "Today?"

"Sooner the better."

"But what are you going to say to him?"

Chip smiled. "I'm gonna tell him he can go ahead and release the damn transcript to the whole world as far as I'm concerned, and that I'm going to play the game of my life tonight. I'm gonna call *his* bluff. Because if he *does* release the transcript and I'm suspended, the game goes off the board and no one can make a bet on it."

"What if that's not his motive?" Susan Carol said. "What if he just wants Duke to win?"

Chip shook his head. "Hell, I could score forty tonight and Duke might still win. In case you hadn't noticed, they're pretty good. Money's involved here, I'm sure of it."

Stevie suddenly felt better. Yeah, he thought, that's the way to do it. Tell the guy to go to hell.

Susan Carol brought him back to earth. "And what if he says, 'Fine, go ahead and play, but the transcript will be in the hands of the media and the NCAA before the trophy is presented,'" she said.

Chip took a deep breath. "I don't know," he said.

Stevie felt the sad and helpless feeling coming back. "So what do we do now?" he said.

"We wait," Chip said. "We wait and hope."

■ ■ ■

They decided to keep their vigil in Chip's hotel room, but it took them almost forty-five minutes to get there because there was so much traffic. Chip kept glancing down at his cell phone as if looking at it would make it ring. They had the cab driver drop them behind the Marriott and went to the back door they had come out of on Sunday morning. It was propped open a couple of inches with a Minnesota State media guide. "Amazing no one ever closes the thing," Chip said, picking up the guide as they walked in. They climbed the stairs to the third floor to avoid running into anyone and took the elevator from there.

They were in the elevator when the cell phone rang. Chip looked at the number and said, "This is it," before he picked it up. He listened for a moment as the elevator reached the forty-first floor.

"That's late," they heard him say, then, "Wait. Let me write down the address." He waved a hand at Stevie and Susan Carol, indicating he needed something to write on. Susan Carol pulled her notebook out and handed it to him with a pen. "And the room number?" he said as he wrote. "Okay. Tell him to be on time. I've got a ball game to play tonight." He paused again. "Of course I'm bringing them. If Jurgensen doesn't like it, tough."

He snapped the phone shut and started walking down the hall toward his room. Stevie started to ask him what had happened, but he shook his head. Looking around, Stevie saw that there were no fewer than four security guards working the hallway, including Mike the Giant. None of them made any move to stop Stevie or Susan Carol as they walked with Chip. Only Mike the Giant said something. "I'm going to let your dad know you're back, Chip," he said.

"Fine," Chip said. "Thanks."

He put the key in the door and they walked inside. As

soon as the door shut, his face lit up with excitement. "Four o'clock at the Days Inn," he said.

"Where's that?" Stevie asked.

"Apparently it's on Canal but up near the highway. Jurgensen got a room there so we'd be away from the crowds."

"Did Feeley give you any idea of whether he might listen to us?" Susan Carol asked.

"No, not really. He just said Jurgensen had said, 'Tell the kid to come on ahead and I'll talk to him.' That's when I told him you guys were coming, too."

Susan Carol sat down in one of the chairs. "Chip, I don't like it. Why meet so late? Why at this out-of-the-way hotel? I don't have a good feeling about this."

"I don't like it, either, but I don't see what choice we have," said Chip. "If you can come up with a better plan in the next few hours, I'm all ears."

■ ■ ■

They spent the afternoon pacing, ordering room service food they couldn't eat, half watching TV, and coming up with impossible alternative plans. Stevie and Susan Carol called to check in with their dads, and luckily neither was in his room. They left messages saying they would be back in time to eat dinner before the game. They didn't even bother with excuses. They decided to worry about that later.

"Lucky for me, Dad made breakfast our pregame," Chip said, picking at the plate of pasta he had ordered.

"Why'd he do that?" Stevie asked.

"He's superstitious. First two games of the tournament,

we played in the afternoon, so we had breakfast. When we won, he decided to keep making breakfast the pregame meal even when we were playing at night. He just told us all to eat something not too heavy before we go to the gym."

"Gym?" Susan Carol said. "You call that Dome a gym?"

Chip laughed. "It's got two baskets and we're playing basketball. So, it's a gym. A big one, but still a gym."

"And what time do you guys leave for the gym?" Susan Carol asked.

"Six-thirty," he said. "It'll be tight, but we'll make it. They need me to play, after all."

Chip called down to the bell desk to get directions to the Days Inn. The bellman told him it would take about twenty minutes on foot or forty minutes by cab—between rush hour and the game, traffic was a mess.

He hung up the phone and smiled at Stevie and Susan Carol. "You guys still up for this?" he said.

"Absolutely," Stevie said, wishing it was time to leave. He was fantasizing about how they were going to tell Jurgensen where he could go with his threats.

"Yes and no," Susan Carol answered.

Stevie and Chip looked at her quizzically.

"I just think we should at least let someone know where we're going," she said. "Jurgensen is clearly not playing games here; he's determined to pull this off—at just about any cost."

"But we've already decided it's too risky to bring in the FBI right now because of the NCAA . . . ," Stevie said.

Susan Carol waved her hand at him. "I know that," she

said. "But let's make sure someone knows where we are and has an idea of what's going on in case something goes wrong over there."

"But who?" Chip said.

"I think Stevie had the right idea earlier. Bobby Kelleher."

"The reporter?" Chip said. "What if he takes the information and goes public with it before the game?"

"He won't do that," Stevie said. "You can't do anything with a story like this without confirmation."

"Plus, he knows about this kind of thing," Susan Carol said. "He broke open that Brickley Shoes scandal. He's not likely to panic in a situation like this."

Chip was starting to come around a little. "So, what do you want to do, call him?"

Susan Carol shook her head. "No. I don't have his cell phone number and I doubt he's in his room. He gave me his e-mail address after the breakfast Friday. He said he checks it every few hours and if I needed anything just to send him an e-mail." She nodded toward the computer set up on a desk across the room. "So we send him an e-mail saying we're working with you to stop a plot to fix the championship game. He's not to say anything to anyone unless by some chance we aren't in the arena by seven o'clock. If we aren't there by then, he's to call the FBI and have Jurgensen and Whiting arrested."

"If I'm not at the arena at seven o'clock, my dad will have the FBI, the CIA, and the entire New Orleans Police Department looking for me," Chip said.

"Good point," Susan Carol said. "But he won't have any idea where to start looking. We'll make sure Kelleher does."

"You really think Jurgensen will try to pull something crazy?" Stevie said.

"No, I don't," Susan Carol said. "But he's clearly not very predictable. Why not cover ourselves?"

Chip nodded. "Okay, I'm convinced. I like the idea of some backup." He smiled. "Boy, I never thought the day would come when I'd feel like the only people I could trust were reporters."

He turned on his computer for Susan Carol and got her signed on, and she quickly typed a message for Kelleher, headed "Important: from writing-contest winners."

"That should get his attention right away," she said. Her note was relatively brief, but it outlined the plot, who the plotters were, and where the meeting was. "Okay?" she said as Chip and Stevie read over her shoulder.

"Send it," Chip said. "And let's get going. It's three-thirty. I want to leave a few extra minutes to get there in case we get lost or have to fight through all the crowds on Bourbon Street." He tugged his cap down low and put on a pair of thick glasses as they walked out the door.

"You wear glasses?" Stevie said.

"Only in big crowds," he said.

He didn't look at all like the floppy-haired kid Stevie had watched play on TV the last few years. "I probably ought to wear a suit and tie," Chip added. "Then not even my dad would recognize me."

The narrow streets were choked with fans, many of them

dueling with fight songs or cheers. It took them about fifteen minutes to get to the other side of the partying section of town. Stevie was initially relieved to be away from the crowds and the screaming but less thrilled when he noticed how seedy their surroundings had become.

"Two more blocks, then we make a left," Chip said in what might have been an attempt to steady everyone's nerves.

"This is the block," Chip said, a couple of minutes later.

They didn't see the Days Inn until they were almost on top of it, because it was hidden by a grove of trees. Stevie was beginning to think it didn't look like such a bad place, but when they walked into the lobby, he realized they were a long way from the Windsor Court. The lobby was tiny, with two chairs and a coffee table on one side and the front desk on the other side.

"Welcome to the other side of New Orleans," Stevie said.

"This is no different than a lot of the places we stay on the road in the Big Ten," Chip said. "You go to West Lafayette, Indiana, or Iowa City, this is about what you get."

He pointed at an elevator bank at the rear of the lobby. "Come on, let's go." They made their way to the designated room.

"Four on the dot," Chip said as they prepared to knock on the door. "You guys ready?"

"More important," Susan Carol said, "are you ready?"

"I hope so," Chip answered as he knocked.

For a split second, Stevie thought no one was inside the

room. Then he heard footsteps. They looked at one another again as if to say, *This is it.*

The door opened and the three of them stood staring at the man who greeted them.

"Right on time," he said. "I'm glad you're all here."

"Where's Jurgensen?" Chip said.

"Come on in and all your questions will be answered," said Dean Benjamin Wojenski.

17: NO WAY OUT

AS SOON AS THEY WALKED INSIDE, Stevie knew they were in trouble. The room was actually some sort of suite, or so he guessed, because there was no bed, just some couches and a desk. There was a door that led to what Stevie guessed was the bedroom.

Tom Whiting was seated, wearing the same sort of sickly smile that Dean Wojenski had been wearing as he ushered them into the room. And standing behind him was Stuart Feeley's assistant, Gary, the muscle-bound flowered-shirt guy.

Chip found his voice first. "Where's Jurgensen?" he asked.

They all laughed, clearly enjoying the confusion on their faces.

"Have a seat," Whiting said, indicating three chairs that had been set up opposite the couch in anticipation of their arrival.

"I think I'll stand," Stevie said. "I may have to leave early to make a phone call."

More laughter. Gary casually pulled a small revolver from underneath his flowered shirt. "Have a seat," he said.

They sat.

"What the hell is going on here?" Chip asked. "We were supposed to meet Steve Jurgensen. Is he coming?"

"Not anytime soon," Dean Wojenski said, sitting on the empty couch against the wall. "But we won't be needing him. His work is done."

"Done?" Chip said. "What do you mean, done?"

"Just done," Wojenski said. "Listen, Chip, we haven't got that long to talk, because we have to get you back to the hotel by . . . what time, Tom?"

"Six-thirty," Whiting said.

"We need to leave before then," Susan Carol said. "If we're not back at our hotel by six o'clock, our dads will worry. They'll probably call the police."

"I doubt it," Dean Wojenski said. "I've already called and left them messages on your behalf saying I'm the editor you are working for tonight and I asked you to leave early for the arena to do a pregame story on the scene over there. But don't worry. You kids aren't in any danger. All Chip has to do is be a good boy tonight and do what he's supposed to do."

"Do what I'm supposed to do? Dean, you're not with . . ."

"Them?" Wojenski said, hooking a thumb toward Whiting and the flower shirt. "More accurately, they're with me."

"But how?" Chip asked. "You helped us identify Jurgensen."

"Yes, I did," Wojenski said. "Once I realized that you weren't going to do the smart thing, I decided to give you a rabbit to chase around while I devised a better plan to ensure your cooperation."

"And what makes you think I'm going to cooperate now?" Chip said.

"Because when you leave for the game in a little while, your friends here are going to stay behind. Gary"—he nodded at the flower shirt—"will stay with them. If all goes well, he'll release them as soon as the game's over. If not . . ."

"You're *crazy*," Chip said. "This is now officially *crazy*. Even if I throw the game tonight, I'll tell the truth tomorrow and nail you guys."

"Oh, I don't think you will. Because then your transcript will be released and the whole litany of unfortunate events will begin. 'I was blackmailed' will sound like a rather creative excuse to cover your failings as both an athlete and a student. No one will believe you.

"No, Chip, you can either lose quietly or lose with a scandal. But you *will* lose."

Stevie was sweating profusely. He looked at Susan Carol, who looked surprisingly calm.

Chip took a deep breath. "Why?" he asked. "You at least owe me that."

Dean Wojenski nodded. "All right. We've got a little time. Gary, get them all drinks. You see? I can be very gracious when I get what I want."

Gary walked into the other room and came back with three cans of Coke. Given how dry Stevie's mouth was, he didn't turn it down.

"I'm surprised you haven't worked it out. It's about money, of course," Dean Wojenski said, glancing at his watch as he began speaking. "I can't take credit for coming up with the idea to blackmail you, Chip, but when the idea was brought to me, I thought it was brilliant."

"Whose idea was it?" Chip said, his voice filled with anger.

"Someone who knew I was once your dean and that I was short on cash. Tom could change your grade in his class, but an earlier failure would give us an unbeatable hand."

"You're a gambler, aren't you?" Susan Carol said.

"Not tonight, my dear," the dean answered.

"And Professor Whiting, why did you get involved?" Chip said. "You'd throw over your school and people who trusted you for a big-money hit?"

"Something like that," Whiting said.

"And you, Gary?" Chip asked.

"Gary's here because someone has to watch your two friends when we leave," Wojenski answered for him. "I must say, the one move you kids made that caught us a little off guard was taking your tale of woe to Stuart. We thought you would go looking for Jurgensen. Fortunately, we were able to turn that to our advantage and here you are."

The three of them looked at one another. They had messed up—big time. They'd gone to Feeley for help and he'd been behind the whole thing. The mastermind was Feeley, or Wojenski, or both.

"I have a question," Susan Carol said.

"What is it, my dear?"

"How much money have you all bet on this game tonight?"

"We've all bet different amounts," Wojenski said. "Each of us bet in different places, and even individually we spread our bets out so no one would get suspicious about a large amount of money coming in on Duke. Tom's work on that gambling commission turned out to be very useful.

"I'm not sure of the exact figure, but I'd estimate our group has about five million at stake tonight. Which means, Chip, that a betrayal on your part would not be taken very well at all."

"That's not to mention—" Whiting said before Wojenski interrupted him.

"No need to mention anything else, Tom," he said. "Chip knows what the consequences will be. Don't you, Chip?"

Chip didn't answer.

Wojenski stood up. "I think the time has come—"

"I've got one more question," Stevie said, half curious and half stalling.

"Yes?" Wojenski said.

"Why tonight? MSU could easily have lost on Saturday and then your whole plan goes down the drain. Why didn't you just make Chip throw Saturday's game?"

Wojenski smiled. "Excellent question, young man. Someday you'll make a very good reporter."

"So what's the answer?" Chip said.

"Too complicated to explain," Wojenski said. "Gary, if you would?"

Gary passed off the revolver to Whiting and produced a roll of duct tape.

"It isn't that we don't think Gary can handle you kids, we just don't want there to be any temptation," Wojenski said as Gary walked behind Stevie and began wrapping tape around his chest and the back of the chair, pinning his arms.

Susan Carol started talking very fast. "You *really* don't want to do this. We told people where we were going. If we don't show up at the game, they'll come here and find us. Then you'll be guilty of kidnapping as well as blackmail. . . ."

But no one seemed to believe her. It sounded like a lie, even to Stevie. Gary continued methodically taping Stevie's ankles to the legs of his chair, and Susan Carol was soon similarly trussed. Wojenski held up two washcloths. "Gary has orders to gag you if necessary, so do be quiet. When the time comes, Gary will let you watch the game. When it's over, you'll be free to go." He turned to Chip. "If—"

"Yeah, yeah," Chip said. "You've made yourself clear."

"I'm not sure I have. Tom will be with you every minute. We also have other people watching you. If you do anything to betray us, we'll be on the phone to Gary within seconds. Any help you try to send would arrive much too late."

Stevie saw Chip redden and start to say something before thinking better of it.

Wojenski smiled an evil smile. "Actually, I should thank you kids," he said. "Chip might have had second thoughts if his transcript was the only thing at risk tonight."

"Ben, we need to get going," Whiting said, passing the gun back to Gary.

"Yes, of course." Wojenski turned to Gary. "If anything goes wrong, Gary, you know what to do."

Gary nodded, sending a chill through Stevie. Even so, as Chip started to go out the door with Whiting in front of him and Wojenski, half-shoving him, right behind, Stevie couldn't stop from yelling at him. "Win the game, Chip!" he said. "Win the game. Don't worry about us! You know Kelleher will find us. He'll be here any minute."

He could hear Susan Carol chiming in. "Listen to Stevie! Win the game!"

Chip looked like he might have tears in his eyes. Wojenski shoved him through the door and turned back to Stevie. "A useless gesture. Make it your last."

He hovered in the doorway a moment before leaving. "Remember," Wojenski said, "you kids are the biggest Duke fans in New Orleans tonight."

■ ■ ■

The two kids tried valiantly to convince Gary that someone really would come for them.

"You don't want to be messed up in this, Gary," tried Susan Carol. "Cancel your bet now and get out while you can."

"Why do *you* have to do the dirty work?" offered Stevie. "You're the one who's going to get caught holding two kids at gunpoint when they get here. You're the one they're going to nail."

But Gary was having none of it. "Quit your yapping" was his only comment, beyond waving the washcloth gag in the air when he wanted them to shut up.

Stevie watched the sky grow dark outside the window. Where the hell was Kelleher? Did he not get the e-mail? Did he not believe them?

He looked over at Susan Carol. Her expression seemed calm, but Stevie noticed a small bead of sweat rolling down her temple.

Susan Carol finally broke the silence by saying, "Gary, can't you at least turn on the TV?"

"Game doesn't start until eight," he said.

"I know," she said. "But we could watch something else?" She gave him her smile.

Stevie wondered if she was up to something. Gary turned the TV to ESPN. "That okay?" he said to Susan Carol.

"Yes, thank you very much," Susan Carol said.

Dick Vitale and Digger Phelps were arguing. Vitale had apparently picked Duke to win the game and Phelps was telling him that he *always* picked Duke. "What's not to like?" Vitale was yelling. "Great coach, great school, great kids . . ."

"But not the best team tonight," Phelps said. "MSU has the best team." He then launched into a breakdown of Minnesota State's offense, all of it coming back to Chip Graber.

"Wow," said Stevie, his voice filled with mock wonder, "sounds like everything is riding on Graber tonight."

Susan Carol snorted. "Yeah, I'll be glued to my chair for this game," she said.

Stevie laughed. "Hey, maybe we should have tried to get an interview with him, huh? That would have been some story."

"I'll say," said Susan Carol. Then, suppressing a giggle, she tried to sound serious. "You know, covering the Final Four hasn't really worked out like I thought it would."

"I know what you mean," responded Stevie, looking down at the duct tape holding him in his chair, then back at Susan Carol. "Don't you hate when that happens?"

They both gave in to hysteria at that, laughing so hard that Gary warned them to shut up. But they couldn't stop—two days' worth of tension was gushing out of them.

■ ■ ■

For the next hour they listened to the game being broken down a thousand different ways. At eight o'clock Vitale and Phelps were replaced on ESPN by a cheerleading championship, and Gary flipped the channel to CBS. Jim Nantz and Billy Packer were telling the audience that this was shaping up to be one of the best championship games in years.

The game started. Open for a three pointer early, Chip drained the shot. "Bad idea," Gary said to the TV. Stevie and Susan Carol looked at one another. Part of Stevie wanted Chip to make every shot he took. Another part of him was terrified by what might happen if he did. Hours had passed. If Kelleher hadn't read their e-mail before the game, it was all over. He sure wasn't going to be checking it *during* the game. . . .

The next ten minutes were hard to watch. Chip wasn't shooting much. Twice he drove to the basket and had his shot blocked. Then he missed a contested three pointer. Two other times down the court, he turned the ball over on the fast break. He did block one J.J. Redick jumper, flying around a screen to deflect the ball. When TV took a time-out with 7:04 to go, Duke was leading 29–20. "It's looking better for you guys," Gary commented.

"Gary, is there any way you could cut the tape on my ankles? My legs are really cramping up," Susan Carol said. Again, the smile and a little bit of a quivering lower lip.

"No." Gary cut her off. "Look, give it up already. You think I'm some stupid—" He stopped abruptly. There was a knock on the door. "You two keep quiet," he hissed. "Who's there?" he said, taking a few quick steps in the direction of the door. Stevie and Susan Carol looked at each other. Help? Should they yell?

Apparently not. Stevie couldn't hear the voice on the other side of the door, but whatever the person said made Gary smile.

"Why didn't you say so?" Gary said. He opened the door a crack.

The next thing Stevie saw was Gary flying backward, the gun sailing out of his hand. A man burst into the room and was on top of him before he could react. The man threw a flurry of punches, making it impossible for Gary to defend himself. After a few seconds, Stevie could see Gary's head drop back onto the carpet. The hulk was out cold.

The man stood up and turned to Stevie and Susan Carol, whose mouths hung open in shock. He was tall, maybe about forty, and obviously stronger than he looked.

"Who are you?" Stevie asked.

"I'm Steve Jurgensen," he said. He strode toward them, pulling out a small pocketknife.

"Are you okay?" he asked as he began to cut them loose from their chairs. "We need to get you to the Dome fast."

18: THE FINAL SHOT

STEVE JURGENSEN had them both free in under a minute. He spotted the roll of duct tape, then dragged Gary, still unconscious, across the room and taped him, quite securely, to the couch. He added a strip of tape over his mouth, then checked to make certain his breathing was normal.

"We can't take any chances on him coming to and making a phone call to warn people," he said. "Can you kids walk all right? Circulation coming back?"

Stevie felt a little bit wobbly, but okay. His back and legs hurt but he knew it would pass. More than anything, he was confused—very confused.

"If you're really Steve Jurgensen," Susan Carol said, rolling her shoulders to loosen up, "why are you rescuing us? You're one of the bad guys."

"Because you're only half right," Jurgensen said. "I am Jurgensen, but I'm not one of the bad guys."

"But you followed us yesterday," Stevie said. "We got the license plate on your car."

"I followed you to try to figure out what Chip was messed up in," Jurgensen said. "Come on. We *have* to get going."

They glanced at the TV. The clock was now under five minutes left in the first half and Duke's lead was 10. If they didn't get to the Dome soon and let Chip know they were all right, MSU was going to get blown out.

He and Susan Carol followed Jurgensen to his car, and they all jumped in the front seat. Jurgensen peeled out of the parking lot but almost immediately screeched to a halt. Even though the game was under way, traffic downtown was still a mess. Jurgensen glanced at his watch. "With luck we can get there before the second half starts."

"Since we have some time," Susan Carol said as Jurgensen hit the brakes again, "maybe you can explain to us what in the world is going on."

Jurgensen nodded. "I'll give it my best shot. Actually, it started when you two kids managed to talk your way in to see Chip Saturday morning."

"How could you possibly know about that?" Stevie said.

"Remember the big guy who stopped you in the hallway?"

"Mike the Giant?"

"Yeah, him. He didn't exactly buy your story even though Chip backed you. He went to Chip's dad and told him about two teenagers visiting Chip, one of them claiming to be Chip's cousin. Well, Alan obviously knew Chip didn't have a cousin in New Orleans. He also knew Chip had been acting kind of funny all week. He hadn't practiced well, which was unlike him. He figured something was going on but didn't know what. He didn't want to confront Chip with it, partly because he thought Chip would come to him when the time was right, but also because they both had a lot on their minds with a Final Four game to play that night. So, he called me."

"Called *you?*" Susan Carol said. "Why, of all people, would Coach Graber call you?"

Jurgensen pulled around a truck that was double-parked on Canal Street. "For one thing, we're friends," he said. "For another, I'm his lawyer."

Stevie and Susan Carol looked at one another, not quite sure what to believe anymore. Up ahead, they could see police lights. There was an accident that was tying traffic up completely. "You're friends with the man who beat you out for the coaching job at Davidson?" Stevie said.

This time Jurgensen laughed. "Who did you hear that story from?"

"Dean Wojenski."

"What does that tell you?"

"That it's a lie," Susan Carol said.

According to Steve Jurgensen, he and Alan Graber had been best friends while assistants at Davidson. When Coach Pritchett left, the original plan was for Jurgensen to go after the job while Graber moved up to become the number one assistant. But Jurgensen hated the hours and, most of all, he hated recruiting.

"I didn't think I could live the rest of my life dependent on the whims of teenagers," he said. "So Alan took the job, and I went into law."

"So when Coach Graber called you Saturday, what did you do?" Susan Carol asked. "What did you know?"

"Not much," Jurgensen said. "Alan just wanted me to keep an eye on Chip, make sure he was okay. My wife happened to mention that Chip was trying to track down Ben Wojenski, so I asked her to be sure he found him."

"So your wife wasn't in on it?" Stevie asked. "Wojenski figured . . ."

"That since Chip had called Christine, I was as good a diversion as any," Jurgensen said. "That's my guess anyway.

"Christine told me you called, Susan Carol, so when I saw you three get in a car the next morning, I figured you were headed out to Bay St. Louis.

"I followed you down there and back, but then you ditched me at the Dome, and I still didn't know what was going on. So I did a little digging into Benjamin Wojenski. Hard to get into public records on a Sunday—unless you know the right people. I found out Wojenski's house is mortgaged to the hilt. So then I got another friend to pull his phone records. Lots of calls to an 800 number that turned out to be an offshore betting service. And then I hit pay dirt."

"How?"

"All sorts of calls to different numbers in the 612 area code and several to a 919 number that I recognized right away."

"Let me guess," Stevie said. "Stuart Feeley."

"You got it."

"And 612 is Minneapolis, right?" Susan Carol said. "Whiting?"

"Right," Jurgensen said. "There were a bunch of calls to Tom Whiting's cell. But it was the other 612 number that was really interesting."

They were now approaching a police checkpoint near the Dome, where police were apparently turning cars away to keep the area around the building clear. Stevie couldn't help but think this was all going to be for nothing if they didn't get moving soon.

They were still a ways from the checkpoint. "Listen, guys, I don't think we can wait any longer," Jurgensen said. He made a hard right turn into a small side street and parked next to a fire hydrant. "We've got to run for it."

He reached into the glove compartment and pulled out three passes marked "All Access."

"Put these on," he said. "You'll need them when we get there."

"But wait," Susan Carol said as they climbed out of the car.

"I'll tell you the rest later," Jurgensen said as they started to run.

"But how'd you know where to find us tonight?" Stevie said.

He could see Jurgensen smile even as they were heading up a hill. "Your e-mail to Bobby Kelleher. Basically, you saved yourselves by sending it. I had no idea where you and

Chip had gone. About seven-thirty I got a nearly hysterical call from Bobby saying he thought you were in trouble."

Stevie took a breath so he could talk. The Dome was now a couple hundred yards away. "Why would Kelleher call you? We told him you were in on it!"

"Luckily, he knows me well enough to know that couldn't be true. So he hoped I'd know what *was* true in your story. Your e-mail had him pretty well floored. But between what you wrote and what I found out, I think we've got it figured."

Stevie glanced at Susan Carol, who seemed to be handling the run a lot better than he and Jurgensen. He wanted to thank her for thinking to send the e-mail to Kelleher. It might have saved their lives. But they were finally approaching the gate of the Superdome, and Stevie had just enough breath to get there.

The guard at the back door seemed very surprised to see anyone with an All Access pass arriving with the second half just under way. But the passes made it impossible for him to question them. All three of them were breathing hard when they made it into the hallway where the locker rooms were. There was almost no one around and they could hear the roar of the game coming from the floor. They sprinted to the tunnel leading to the floor. Across the way they could see a scoreboard. Duke was leading 59–50, with just under twelve minutes to play.

"We have to get you guys someplace where we can be sure Chip will see you," Jurgensen said.

"Well," Stevie said, "we've got All Access passes. Next

time-out, we just walk over near the bench and get his attention coming out of the huddle."

Jurgensen nodded. "That should work."

They walked to the end of the tunnel that put them just yards from the MSU bench. They stood off to one side and waited for the whistle to stop play. "One more thing, real quick," Susan Carol said, still panting a bit. "How did you get Gary to open the door for you?"

Jurgensen smiled. "I told him I was the hotel manager and I had champagne sent by Mr. Feeley for a postgame celebration."

"Nice," Stevie said.

"Thought of it in the car on the way over," he said. "I was counting on there only being one guy guarding you. And I wasn't counting on that *gun*. I was lucky."

"We all were," said Susan Carol.

They heard a whistle. TV was going to time-out with 10:59 left. Duke's lead was 63–53.

As the players came to the bench and sat down facing away from the crowd, Stevie and Susan Carol started to make a move. "Hang on," Jurgensen said. "You go too soon, he'll be looking the wrong way. Wait until you hear the first horn."

During time-outs, there were two horns. The first one told the players and coaches they had thirty seconds to get back on court. The second sounded with ten seconds left and the officials would go into the huddle to break it up if the players were still lingering.

"As soon as you hear the first horn, move very quickly,"

Jurgensen said. "Walk right up to the scorer's table, because the ball is at the other end and Chip will go right past there."

They nodded. And waited. Finally they heard the horn. "Go!" Jurgensen said.

Stevie started running, Susan Carol right behind him. They were past the guard protecting the area behind the bench in an instant, Stevie yelling, "All Access!" as they went by.

He heard a voice say, "Hey, stop them, stop those kids!"

He didn't have to turn around to recognize who it was, because the voice was now familiar to him: Tom Whiting. He heard other people yell and then saw Chip turn in the direction of the commotion. He stopped as Chip turned around and, as loud as he could to be heard over the din, screamed, "We're okay, Chip, we're okay!" Susan Carol was jumping up and down behind him, waving her arms and screaming, too.

Chip saw them and smiled, but just as he did, two security guards grabbed Stevie and Susan Carol. Chip started over to say something, but the second horn went off and the officials were screaming at the MSU players to get back on court. Chip hesitated. "Go play!" Stevie yelled. "Just go and win the game!"

If he was dragged away now, it was okay. The guard was pulling him backward when he heard another voice say, "Let them go. They've got All Access passes. Let them go right now."

The voice belonged to Coach Alan Graber. It suddenly

occurred to Stevie that they had never asked Jurgensen where he had gotten the All Access passes. Now he knew. "They're with us," he heard Alan Graber saying. "Just let them go. They're fine."

The security guards looked confused. But they didn't argue. They let go and backed away.

"Come on, Stevie," Susan Carol said. "Let's get out of here."

That was fine with Stevie. Coach Graber smiled at them, then turned back to the court, where his team was inbounding the ball. Whiting, seated on the end of the bench, was glaring at them. But he couldn't say anything. He couldn't overrule his coach. Stevie wanted to say something as he walked past, but resisted. They had gotten the message to Chip. The rest was up to him.

■ ■ ■

Stevie and Susan Carol tried to find Jurgensen, but he wasn't in the hallway where they'd left him. Then they looked for Kelleher on press row, but he wasn't in his seat. So they reclaimed their own seats in the overflow press section with less than six minutes to play. Those last minutes of the game might have been the most emotional moments of Stevie's life. They'd been watching Chip slowly take control of the game. Stevie could see on the scoreboard that Graber now had 19 points. Duke's lead was down to 73–69. "He caught his second wind a few minutes ago," one of the writers sitting next to them said. "It's like someone just turned him on."

MSU and Duke went back and forth in the final minutes. Chip tied the score at 80 with an off-balance driving layup with fourteen seconds left. Krzyzewski called time to set up a final play. "I'm not sure I can sit through another overtime," Susan Carol said. "But I hope they don't score."

Stevie knew she meant it. His heart was pounding yet again. The time-out seemed to take forever. Finally, the teams were back on the court.

Duke inbounded. Everyone in the building knew the ball was going to J.J. Redick, their brilliant shooter. Terry Armstrong, the point guard, held the ball near midcourt as the clock went down. Everyone in the arena was standing. As the clock went down to five seconds, Stevie saw Redick sprinting around a screen near the top of the key. Armstrong snapped a pass in his direction. But it never got there. Out of nowhere came Chip. He'd been guarding Duke's other superb shooter, Daniel Ewing, but had gambled at the last minute and left him alone. Chip got his hand on the ball and deflected it toward midcourt.

Stevie could see the clock clicking from :03 to :02 as Chip picked the ball up in full flight, Armstrong sprinting back to cut him off. Chip was almost at the exact same spot where he had made the winning shot on Saturday, when he stopped his dribble and went up in the air to shoot. Armstrong was diving at him, screaming at the top of his lungs, "No, no, no way!"

Just as Chip released the ball, Armstrong piled into him and they both went down to the floor. Stevie wondered if there would be a foul call, but he heard no whistle. Stevie thought he must be watching a replay of the end of the St.

Joe's game. This time, though, the ball hit the back of the rim and bounced high into the air. Overtime, Stevie thought. But then the ball dropped down, hit the front of the rim, hung there for a moment, and dropped through the net.

Bedlam.

Stevie knew he was jumping up and down and screaming and acting completely unprofessional. He didn't care. Someone was pounding him and hugging him. It was Susan Carol. She had tears in her eyes. Well, so did he. It was déjà vu all over again. Same spot on the court, almost the same shot.

Chip had disappeared completely under a pile of his celebrating teammates. Stevie saw Krzyzewski waiting patiently for the pile to clear so he could congratulate him. Grudgingly, he had to concede that was a pretty classy move.

Suddenly Jurgensen appeared at their seats. "Come on," he said. "We've got work to do."

They followed him to the tunnel. People were running in all directions, shouting instructions at one another. They were right underneath the Duke section, which was the one place in the Dome that wasn't going completely crazy. At the top of the tunnel, Stevie saw a half dozen men in suits.

"Thanks for coming, Rick," Jurgensen said, shaking hands with one of them, a tall bald man who did not appear likely to smile anytime soon.

"Steve, I came because your word has always been good in the past," Rick said. "I'm assuming it's good now, although that's a wild story you told me on the phone."

"It's all true," Jurgensen said. "These are the two kids I told you about. Stevie, Susan Carol, this is Special Agent Rick Applebaum. He runs the New Orleans field office of the FBI. We've worked together on cases in the past."

They all shook hands. "You kids okay?" Applebaum said. They nodded. "And are you *sure* Graber will talk?" he said, eyes fixed on Jurgensen.

"He'll talk. And so will these two. You'll have plenty. And I can testify to seeing them tied up at the hotel."

"Yeah, we've already picked up the guy you left back there," Applebaum said. "Nice tape job. Okay, let's go get the rest of them."

Jurgensen told them where everyone was likely to be: Whiting on court with the team, Feeley in the Duke section. "And you'll find Koheen down on the floor trying to look happy about the outcome," he said.

Koheen? Stevie knew the name but wasn't sure from where. Then he remembered the MSU media guide. Susan Carol had figured it out a split second before him. "Earl Koheen?" she said. "The president of MSU?"

Jurgensen nodded. "That's the part I didn't get to tell you. The other calls Wojenski made to the 612 area code were to Earl Koheen. It took me a while to add things up, but in the end, it all connects."

"Wait a minute," Stevie said. "The media guide. It said that one of Koheen's professors at Providence was . . ."

"Tom Whiting," Susan Carol said, finishing the sentence for him.

"And guess who was teaching up there at the exact same time," Jurgensen said.

Stevie and Susan Carol looked at one another. Something Wojenski had said came back to Stevie. He'd said he and his wife were both from Rhode Island.

"Wojenski," he said.

"Right," Jurgensen said. "That's where it all clicked. Koheen has been quietly sniffing around all winter to replace Tom Sanford as Duke's president. I knew that from being on the board. Then all of a sudden MSU and Duke are in the Final Four. Koheen knew Chip had been in some academic trouble and he also knew that Feeley's finances hadn't been great the last year or so. My guess is he called Feeley and offered a deal: I'll see to it that Duke wins the championship game if the schools play. Feeley makes a huge financial hit and in return Koheen ends up as Duke's president."

"And Whiting goes along with him to a big job at Duke, right?" Susan Carol said. "That explains why the fix had to be on this game. It *wasn't* just about the money."

"Right. And Koheen and Whiting knew that Wojenski had always had gambling problems even when he was still working. They were certain he would help set up the scheme."

"Wojenski?" Applebaum said. "Where is he?"

They all looked at one another. "He might be with Whiting or Koheen," Jurgensen said. "Come on, we'll point everyone out to you."

They all walked to the court. The FBI men, Stevie

noticed, wore All Access passes that had apparently been produced for them very quickly. Heads turned as they made their way to the floor. Things happened very fast. Whiting was standing to the side watching the celebration when an agent approached him. He didn't even look surprised. Jurgensen led Applebaum directly to President Koheen, who was standing next to Bob Bowlsby, whom Stevie recognized as the chairman of the NCAA men's basketball committee. Stevie was trailing Jurgensen and Applebaum. Susan Carol had gone with another agent to identify Feeley.

"Earl Koheen?" Stevie heard Applebaum say.

Koheen gave Applebaum a puzzled look. Apparently, no one had warned him that he might be in trouble.

"My name is Rick Applebaum. I am the special agent in charge of the New Orleans field office of the FBI. Sir, you are under arrest."

"Arrest?" Bowlsby said, clearly stunned.

"Yes, sir. Mr. Koheen—"

"*Doctor* Koheen," the about-to-be-disgraced president said.

"Okay, *Doctor* Koheen," Applebaum said without even a hint of a smile in the face of Koheen's arrogance. "Doctor Koheen, you are under arrest for attempted blackmail, for tampering with state records, and for conspiracy to kidnap two minors."

"That's a complete lie," Koheen said. "If you lay a hand on me, you will be subjected to the lawsuit of your life."

"I'll take my chances," Applebaum said.

He turned Koheen not-so-gently away from him so he

could handcuff him. Stevie was suddenly aware of dozens of photographers, on court to photograph the awards ceremony and net-cutting, turning their attention to the sight of Koheen in handcuffs. Koheen screamed, "Stop them! Someone stop them! Someone call my lawyer!"

Applebaum led him across the court, with Stevie following, trying not to get trampled by the photographers. He saw Bill Brill and Dick Weiss standing at the corner of the court, their mouths open wide, as Koheen was led past them. A few yards away, coming from the stands, he saw another agent with Feeley and Susan Carol.

"Stevie, what in the world is going on here?" Weiss said. "Where were you all night?"

"Long story," Stevie said. "I'll tell you later."

He raced up the tunnel. Security people were blocking all the media—reporters and photographers—telling them they had to go to the other side of the court to exit. But the security wall parted as soon as Stevie got near. He wasn't sure if it was his pass or if Applebaum had said something.

At the top of the tunnel, Stevie saw Whiting and Feeley and Koheen all in cuffs and surrounded by FBI guys. Susan Carol and Jurgensen were waiting to one side, and as Stevie joined them he heard footsteps behind them: Bobby Kelleher.

"So I guess Steve got there in time," Kelleher said, shaking hands with Stevie and Susan Carol. "I saw you guys come running in during the time-out, but I didn't have a chance to come and talk to you. Steve and I were calling in the FBI. We need to have a long, long talk."

Susan Carol nodded. "We certainly owe you that—and a lot more," she said.

Kelleher shook his head. "You don't owe me anything. You saved yourselves—and the Final Four. I was just the messenger."

"No sign of Wojenski anyplace," one of the agents said, coming up behind Kelleher.

"These guys say he never came to the game tonight," said another.

"Send a car to his home," Applebaum said. "If he's not there, put out an APB. Let's get these guys booked. *Doctor* Koheen wants to call his lawyer."

He turned to Jurgensen. "I'll need you and the kids and the Grabers and Kelleher in my office tomorrow morning for complete statements."

"No problem," Jurgensen said.

Applebaum turned to Stevie, Susan Carol, and Kelleher. "I know you two are aspiring journalists. And I know, Mr. Kelleher, that you are sitting on quite a story here. I can't order you to do anything. But I'm *asking* all three of you not to write about this tonight or talk to anyone else in the media. Once you've given me your statements, it will be different. Do you understand?"

Stevie and Susan Carol both nodded. Not Kelleher.

"You don't expect us not to write about all these arrests, do you?" he said. "I have to write that the president of MSU was led away in handcuffs minutes after his team won the national championship, and I have to explain why."

Applebaum nodded. "I know that, Kelleher," he said. "I

just don't want the kids sitting down and telling you their whole story until they've talked to us first."

"That's not a problem," Kelleher said. "I understand."

Applebaum waved his hand at the entourage of agents and arrestees. "Joe," he said to the agent standing nearest him, "you get these guys to our office. Call the U.S. Attorney's office and have someone meet you there. I'm going to stay behind to brief the Grabers before they speak to the media."

Joe nodded and led the way down the hall. There was a throng of screaming reporters and photographers to walk through before they could exit, but the three distinguished gentlemen in handcuffs were like a little bubble of silence, passing through the storm.

19: TELLING THE STORY

ONCE THE AWARDS CEREMONY WAS OVER, Alan and Chip Graber had to attend the postgame press conference. And, exciting as the game and the win had been, it was impossible to get around the fact that the president of Minnesota State had been taken off the court in handcuffs by an FBI agent in the midst of the postgame victory celebration.

"I'm not a hundred percent certain what happened or why it happened," Alan Graber said. "I'm told it will all come out tomorrow. For right now, I'd like to stick to questions about the game, about us winning the national championship, and about what our team and my son just accomplished."

Chip wore the net into which his final shot had dropped around his neck. He explained his lackluster play in the first thirty minutes as a combination of nerves and good defense played by Duke. Stevie and Susan Carol were standing in the back of the interview room with Steve Jurgensen and Bobby Kelleher, listening. Dick Weiss and Bill Brill walked over to join them.

"You guys know about this," Weiss said. "You tried to tell us before . . ."

Kelleher answered for them. "They do, Hoops," he said. "But they can't tell you what's going on tonight. Tomorrow, like Alan just said, it will all come out."

Weiss and Brill looked at each other. "You guys promise you'll fill us in tomorrow?" Brill said.

"Absolutely," Stevie said.

"Everything we know," said Susan Carol.

When the press conference was over, they went around to the curtained-off area of the hallway that was used to transport the players and coaches to and from the interview room. Again, no one stopped them when they walked behind the curtain. The All Access passes seemed to make the security people magically disappear when they approached. Roger Valdiserri was sitting there in his golf cart, waiting for the Grabers, who had stopped to talk to a couple of NCAA types as they left the podium. As soon as Chip saw Stevie and Susan Carol, he broke into a run. When he got to them, he gathered them both into a hug.

"We did it! *You* did it!" he said. Stevie could see he had tears in his eyes.

"That was a hell of a last shot," Stevie said.

"What happened? How'd you get here?" asked Chip.

"It was Mr. Jurgensen—it's all thanks to him," said Susan Carol.

"Not true," Jurgensen said. "Your e-mail to Kelleher saved the day."

Chip shook hands with Jurgensen. "Dad told me a little about what you did," he said. "I'm glad to meet you."

"So, do I finally get to meet these two young heroes?"

It was Alan Graber, walking up behind his son. Chip introduced them. "You know, it all turned out okay in the end," Alan Graber said. "But if you'd come to me right away, Chipper—"

"It turned out better than fine in the end," Jurgensen broke in. "All those people wouldn't be going to jail if Chip hadn't handled it the way he did."

"Or if Stevie and Susan Carol hadn't overheard me on Friday," Chip said.

"But Chip," Stevie said, "you made your first three-pointer and then you basically stopped shooting. What was going on?"

Chip smiled. "I told myself Kelleher would get your message and get to you. But as soon as I made that shot, a chill went through me. What if I'm wrong? I kept trying to convince myself you'd be okay, but I couldn't shake the vision of you tied to those chairs. . . ."

"So you weren't actually throwing the game."

"Not really. I just couldn't concentrate. Once I saw you, I was okay. And then I got really *mad*. I decided that, one way or the other, we *had* to win."

"And you did," Susan Carol said, her eyes sparkling.

Chip put an arm around Susan Carol. "We did," he said. "But I'm sorry about your Dukies."

She smiled. "I was rooting for you all the way, Chip. But don't tell Coach K." She grinned at Stevie. "They'll be back next year, right, Stevie?"

Stevie nodded. "They probably will," he said. "And if they don't play someone from Philly, I might root for them."

She leaned over and kissed him on the cheek. "Then again, you might not."

■ ■ ■

The one thing Stevie and Susan Carol had left to do that night was explain to their fathers what had been going on. They sat in a corner of the all-night coffee shop at the hotel and laid the whole thing out as their dads sat with their mouths agape. Both of them insisted that they should have come to them and told them what was going on, but it was pretty clear they were both relieved their kids were okay and also quite proud of them.

"Do me one favor," Bill Thomas said to Stevie. "Tell your mother that I knew exactly where you were at all times."

Reverend Anderson laughed. "Ditto that for your mother, Susan Carol," he said.

■ ■ ■

The newspapers the next morning reported the arrests of four men in connection with a conspiracy to blackmail a player. There were few details other than the names of the four men arrested and a quote from Rick Applebaum saying that another conspirator was still at large. Which meant they hadn't found Dean Wojenski.

Stevie heard a report on CNN saying that the *Washington Herald*—Kelleher's paper—was reporting that the blackmail conspiracy involved Chip Graber and that two teenaged reporters had helped break the case open for the FBI. Stevie liked hearing that. And Kelleher deserved to be ahead on the story, that was for sure.

Their dads took them to the FBI field office at nine o'clock the next morning, where they gave their statements. It was almost lunchtime by the time they were finished. Chip and Alan Graber were still there, too. Agent Applebaum explained that there had been no sign of Dean Wojenski in Bay St. Louis. His wife had told the agents that as soon as Chip's shot went through the hoop, he had snapped off the television, gone upstairs, packed a bag, and told her he had to leave town for a while. She kept asking the agents to tell her what was going on. Stevie felt bad for her.

"We'll find him," Applebaum said. "Sooner or later."

"How strong is the case?" Bill Thomas asked. "If it comes down to Chip and the kids against the president of a university and the chairman of the board of trustees at Duke . . ."

Applebaum waved a hand. "It won't. Please don't say this publicly but Feeley has already confessed. He gave it all up last night, said he should never have gotten involved."

"Why'd he do it, then?" asked Stevie.

"He said it seemed like easy money and his school would be guaranteed a national championship as a bonus. And I think he was looking forward to having Duke's new president in his pocket. But anyway, he's talking. Plus, Whiting has made it pretty clear he'll do anything to stay out of jail. So if he testifies against Koheen, we'll probably cut him a deal."

"But *shouldn't* he go to jail?" Stevie asked.

"They should all do time," Applebaum said. "But we have the least firsthand evidence against Koheen. We probably need Whiting's testimony."

They were all led to a room that had been set up for a press conference. Before they went in, Stevie asked if Agent Applebaum could send someone to find out if Bill Brill and Dick Weiss were there, and if so, could they see them before they had to go inside. When Brill and Weiss were brought back, Stevie and Susan Carol told them that they would tell them everything after the press conference was over.

"Bill and I have talked," Weiss said. "We have a better idea. Why don't you two guys write your own story and we'll run it in our newspapers under your byline."

Stevie and Susan Carol looked at their dads. "I've already changed our flight to tomorrow morning," Bill Thomas said.

"Same with me," Reverend Anderson said.

"Then let's do it," Susan Carol said.

Stevie turned to Chip. "So are we on the record *now*, Chip?"

Chip laughed. "Completely on the record. The whole story. You guys are the only ones who know it all."

Alan Graber looked at Chip. "You ready to go in there?" he said.

"Ready if you are," Chip said.

"You two kids ready?" Applebaum asked.

"Reporters aren't supposed to be part of the story," Susan Carol said.

Stevie laughed. "At least they won't call us student-athletes," he said.

"You know what?" Alan Graber said. "You guys shouldn't just write a story about all this," he said. "You should write a book."

Susan Carol nodded, grinning. "What do you think, Stevie, should we do a book together?"

"I think we should probably get good at writing newspaper stories first," he said.

She leaned down and said softly, "But you're *already* good at that."

"Don't start with me, Scarlett," he said.

She gave him the smile. "Let's go get this over with so we can write."

That sounded good to Stevie. Just about perfect, in fact. They followed Applebaum and the Grabers onto the podium and into the glare of the TV lights.

Stevie knew he had been right about one thing from the beginning: this would *not* be his last Final Four. And now he knew one other thing for sure: there would *never* be another one quite like this one.

At least he hoped not.

Don't miss
Stevie and Susan Carol covering
the U.S. Open Tennis Tournament
in *Vanishing Act*.

4: NADIA SYMANOVA

"So, what's the scouting report on Evelyn Rubin?" Bobby Kelleher asked. "I see she made Boo-Hoo Three cry."

"Stevie's in love with her," Susan Carol reported.

"I am *not!*" Stevie said. "She's pretty and she seemed nice. That doesn't mean I'm in love. She can really play, though. Great ground strokes, and she's fast."

Susan Carol was grinning. "*And* a beautiful smile."

"An older woman, huh, Stevie?" Kelleher said, smiling. Without giving Stevie a chance to respond, he gestured at the TV screen propped on the corner of his desk. "The match before Symanova out on Armstrong is just about over. If you guys want good seats, we probably ought to walk over there."

"Do we have time to eat something?" Susan Carol said.

Kelleher shook his head. "No. If you want to eat, we probably won't get into the press section."

"I'm not that hungry," Stevie said.

"That figures," Susan Carol answered, rolling her eyes.

"Bud wants to come too," Kelleher said. "In fact, he might have a sandwich or something—he's always carrying food."

Kelleher turned out to be right. Collins was more than happy to offer up a choice of sandwiches. Stevie and Susan Carol each grabbed one and quickly disposed of them. They grabbed cups of Coke and made their way back outside. The temperature had gone up at least ten degrees and the number of people appeared to have doubled. Kelleher led the way, with Stevie and Susan Carol behind him and Collins, hat pulled low over his head, right behind them. Even with the cap, people were constantly screaming Collins's name. He answered everyone but kept moving, his hand on Stevie's shoulder to make sure he stayed close to him.

"Gotta keep moving!" he said. "If Nadia's boyfriend isn't there when the match starts, she'll be very upset."

"Where? Who?" everyone kept asking.

"Right here in front of me," Collins would reply. "Young Steven Thomas. Don't you read the tabloids?"

Given that Symanova was three years older than Stevie and about a half-foot taller, the notion of them as an item was pretty outrageous. But such was the power of Bud that few fans seemed skeptical. One woman wearing a tennis dress even asked Stevie for his autograph. "Not right now," Collins said. "After the match. He's got his game face on."

They made it to the entrance and walked under the stands to the far side, where a small sign with an arrow said MEDIA SEATING. They went up a short flight of steps and came out in a section that was almost directly behind the court—which was empty at the moment. Apparently the prior match had ended. The stands were almost full and there were no more than ten seats left in the media seating area, which Stevie estimated had about 150 seats.

"Just in time," Kelleher said.

A security guard stood at the top of the steps checking badges. He gave Stevie a skeptical look and twice looked at the photo on Stevie's badge and then back at him. Having been through the same sort of thing at the Final Four, Stevie said nothing. When the guard went back for a third look, Kelleher couldn't take it. "You can look at the photo a hundred times and it's going to be him," he said. "He's working with me. He's legit."

"Whaddya think, workin' with you makes the kid legit?" the guard said in one of those unmistakable New York accents. "I'm just doin' my job here, okay?"

"Fine," Kelleher said. "Are you done doing your job now?"

"You want I should just throw youse bot' out?" the guard said.

Before Kelleher could respond, Collins, a step behind Kelleher, jumped in. "Fellas, fellas, let's all be friends here," he said. "Mr. . . . ?"

"Shapiro," the guard said. "Max Shapiro."

"Max, nice to meet you," Collins said, shaking hands with

the guard as if they were long-lost friends. "This is Bobby Kelleher. He's the leading tennis writer in the country, and this is his assistant, Steven Thomas. They're just like you and me, here to see Symanova. No one wants any trouble."

Shapiro eyed Stevie and Kelleher for another moment. "Okay, Bud," he said. "Seein' that it's you, okay. But the kid don't look older than thirteen."

"Well, they do get younger-looking all the time," Collins said.

That seemed to satisfy Max, who moved aside. Stevie heard someone several rows up shouting Kelleher's name.

"Kelleher, right here—I was about to give up on you guys!"

Stevie looked in the direction of the voice—which was very familiar—and did a double take. It was Mary Carillo, the CBS tennis commentator who he knew also worked for ESPN. His dad had told him on more than one occasion that if his mother ever ran off with George Clooney, the first person he would pursue was Carillo.

Carillo had black hair and big brown eyes. Her distinctively deep voice sounded exactly as it did on television.

"The love of my life," she said, throwing her arms around Kelleher as they walked up to greet her. "Only for you and Bud would I have fought off the masses to save these seats. Who've we got here?"

Kelleher introduced her to Susan Carol and Stevie. "I can't tell you what a big fan I am," Susan Carol said. "I love listening to you talk about tennis."

"Learned it all from the master," Carillo said, hugging Collins. "Right, master?"

"You never needed to learn a thing," Collins said. "You were born knowing everything about tennis."

Stevie, feeling a little bit left out, heard himself blurt, "My dad thinks you're hot."

Carillo laughed, a musical laugh that was filled with joy. "Thank you, Stevie," she said. "I will take that as a compliment. And tell your dad thank you."

They all maneuvered into the seats Carillo had apparently saved for them. Others were right behind them searching for fast-filling seats.

"How soon?" Kelleher said, settling in between Carillo and Stevie.

"They announced players on court to warm up at two o'clock," Carillo said. "I've got one-fifty-five. Hey, did you see the Rubin kid beat Boo-Hoo Three? She could play Symanova in the third round."

"Didn't see it," Kelleher said. "But Susan Carol and Stevie did."

"What'd you think?" Carillo said, turning to Stevie as if they were peers.

Feeling quite expert, Stevie said, "Well, she's very good from the back of the court, but she doesn't volley at all."

"Sweetie, no one volleys in women's tennis," Carillo said in a tone that somehow didn't sound like a put-down, even though he knew she was right.

"We haven't had a true serve-and-volleyer since Martina," Collins said.

A murmur ran through the crowd and Stevie saw a TV cameraman backing out of the tunnel that was right in the middle of the stands across from the umpire's chair. A moment later, a security guy came out onto the court followed by a short, dark-haired player carrying an enormous racquet bag who Stevie knew had to be Joanne Walsh, Symanova's opponent. Stevie knew nothing about her other than what he had seen in the newspaper that morning. She was twenty-four years old and ranked ninety-sixth in the world. The paper had referred to her as a "veteran," which in women's tennis meant anyone over twenty-one. A second security man walked right behind Walsh.

Stevie realized he was standing up, craning his neck for a view of Symanova. Walsh kept walking across the court to the players' chairs but the cameraman remained poised just outside the tunnel waiting for Symanova.

"Where is she?" Susan Carol asked. The crowd was beginning to buzz. Walsh had reached her seat and was unzipping her racquet bag. Still, no one else came out of the tunnel.

"Maybe she stopped to check her makeup," Collins said.

Kelleher laughed. "There is that little bathroom right off the court."

"Yeah," Carillo said. "Remember when this was the stadium court and Lendl used to jump in there and change so he could go straight to the parking lot without going back to the locker room?"

"We used to call him Ivan the Unshowered," Collins said.

The buzz was growing. Still, there was no sign of Symanova. Walsh was now standing, holding her racquet, looking up at the umpire. The umpire had put her hand over the microphone and was leaning down to talk to Walsh.

"This is now officially getting strange," Carillo said.

"Check this out," Collins said, pointing in the direction of the tunnel.

A gaggle of security men came sprinting from the tunnel—Stevie counted one, two, three, four, five of them—followed by two men in blazers, both of them barking into walkie-talkies.

"Uh-oh," Kelleher said. "Something's up, something big-time."

"She must be hurt," Collins said. "But how do you get hurt walking over to the court?"

"Tripped on her stilettos?" Susan Carol asked.

"She's wearing sneakers!" Stevie said, thinking that was a dumb comment until he realized she was being sarcastic. "Nice, she's hurt and you're making jokes."

"Calm down, Stefano, I'm sure your betrothed is fine," Collins said, smiling.

The new group of security men had gone directly to Walsh and spoken to her. Whatever they said, she walked quickly back to her chair, zippered her racquet back into her bag, and began walking back across the court with no fewer than eight blue-shirted security men surrounding her. Seeing this, the crowd began whistling—the tennis equivalent of booing.

"Walsh is leaving," Stevie said. "Symanova must be hurt."

Kelleher was shaking his head. "If she's hurt, what's with all the security people around Walsh? Something's up. Come on, guys, we need to get out of here."

"*Now?*" Susan Carol said.

"Yup," Kelleher said, "right now."

He pointed at the two walkie-talkie guys, who were talking intently to the umpire. "Soon as they make an announcement, all hell is going to break loose here. We need to get moving so we don't get trapped in the stampede for the exits. Come on."

"I need to stay," Carillo said. "I'll see you guys later."

"I better stay too," Collins said. "You young guns start chasing this down."

Kelleher shrugged and made his way to the aisle. Stevie kind of wanted to stay too, but he trusted Kelleher's instincts. Susan Carol seemed to agree, because she was standing, clearly ready to move. The three of them started down the steps while others in the media section were standing up and consulting with one another. They bolted past Max Shapiro and down the steps leading under the stadium. They were under the stands and sprinting through an almost empty concourse when they heard what had to be the umpire's voice on the PA system. She wasn't calling out any score.

"Ladies and gentlemen, we regret to announce that the scheduled match between Joanne Walsh and Nadia Symanova has been postponed until a later time." Stevie could hear groans and shouts coming from inside as the umpire forged on. "More details will be announced when they become available. Thank you for your patience and indulgence."

Kelleher turned to Stevie and Susan Carol, shaking his head. "There's *nothing* in the rules about postponing a match. If she's hurt, she defaults. Something crazy's going on here."

They made it out onto the courtyard between the two stadiums. There were security people and police all over the place, blocking the most direct path back to the main stadium. When a security guard stopped Kelleher, he held up his media badge. "We're media," he said. "We have to get back to the media center."

"I don't care who you are," the security man said. "You can go through the food court like everyone else and you'll get there eventually. This area's frozen right now."

Stevie could see two cops right behind the security guy, ready to back him up. People were being herded from the area very quickly by security and police, all of them being pushed toward the food court. Kelleher could clearly see this was an argument he wasn't going to win—even if Collins had been there.

He took one swipe at getting something accomplished. "Can't you at least tell us what in the world is going on?" he said.

One of the cops answered, stepping in front of the security guard. "Here's what I can tell you, pal: if you don't get moving right now, you're going to jail. How's that for telling you something?"

Stevie could see Kelleher redden a little and bite his lip. He turned to Stevie and Susan Carol. "Come on," he said, pointing them toward the food court. The good news was that because they had beaten the crowd out of Louis Armstrong, they were able to maneuver their way through the food court fairly quickly.

Kelleher pulled open the door that led back inside with

a frustrated yank. The scene inside the building was chaotic. People were running in and out of the entrance to the media center shouting, as far as Stevie could tell, in a variety of languages.

"Okay," Kelleher said, pausing just outside the pressroom entrance. "We need a strategy of some kind. I think we should split up . . ."

He broke off in midsentence as a middle-aged man with graying hair ducked out of the media center and made a quick turn away from them.

"Arlen!" Kelleher said, heading toward the man. "Arlen, hang on a second!"

The man half turned, still walking, and waved a hand as if to say, go away. "Not now, Bobby. I can't talk. We're organizing a press conference. We'll let you know what's going on in a while."

He had slowed down enough that Kelleher was able to catch up to him. Stevie and Susan Carol followed at what they hoped was a discreet distance.

"In a while?" Kelleher said. "Come on, Arlen, give me a break. Don't give me that press conference crap. What happened out there? Where the hell is Symanova?"

The man stopped and turned to face Kelleher. Stevie noticed he was quite pale. He looked around as if to be sure no one could hear him and dropped his voice to a whisper so that Stevie, standing right behind Kelleher, could barely hear.

"We don't know," he said.

For a second, Kelleher just stared at him. "What do you mean you don't know? How can you not know? Wasn't she on her way over to Armstrong with Walsh?"

"*Yes,* she *was!*" Arlen said, clearly exasperated, still looking around as if he was afraid someone would hear him. "They were on their way over there and she disappeared."

"*Disappeared!*" Kelleher shouted.

"Bobby, please," Arlen hissed, signaling Kelleher to keep his voice down. "Yes, she disappeared. You know what it's like out there between the stadiums. We had four security guys surrounding the two players. A group of people cut across their path headed for the food court. The security guys got jostled. Walsh and her two guys kept going—no one bumped them. By the time Symanova's guys got untangled, she was gone."

"But how is that possible?"

Arlen held up his hand. "For crying out loud, Bobby, if we knew, she wouldn't be missing, would she? We've sealed all the exits to the place, but that's the problem—we're right on the edge of a park. There are plenty of ways to get off the property without walking through an exit." He looked around again. "I've got to go. There's a meeting in about two minutes. I've told you everything I know."

"Okay, okay," Kelleher said. "Can I quote you on this stuff?"

Arlen smiled wanly. "At this point, that's the least of my worries." He turned and walked down the hallway.

"Who was that?" Stevie asked.

"Arlen Kanterian," Kelleher said. "He's the CEO of professional tennis for the U.S. Tennis Association. It means he's in charge of the tournament. He talks to me because his brother Harry's a friend of mine." He took a deep breath.

"Okay, this story is officially huge. Beyond huge. We've got a big leg up on people right now—let's do something with it."

"Like what?" Susan Carol said, for once looking as baffled as Stevie felt.

Kelleher took another deep breath. "Good question," he said. Then he snapped his fingers. "Listen, Susan Carol, *you* can get into the junior girls' locker room."

"What's that?" she asked.

"I'll give you the short version," Kelleher said. "There are so many girls under eighteen in the event that they have a separate locker room that the media isn't allowed into. Since female reporters are allowed in the men's locker room, male reporters are allowed into the women's. But not where there are women under the age of eighteen. It's been a huge controversy for years because all the players freak out about us being in the locker room. The point is the junior locker room door's not even marked, and they usually don't even have a guard on it because they don't want to call attention to it. If you take your press credential off, you can probably walk in there like you're a player."

"How do *you* know where it is?" Susan Carol said.

"Carillo showed me. Come on, let's start walking. I'll show you where it is. Meantime, Stevie, I want you in the players' lounge. Once you're past the guard, take your credential off and just walk around and listen. I'm going to the men's locker room. We'll meet back here in thirty minutes."

"What exactly are we listening for?" Stevie asked as they started to walk down the long hallway.

Kelleher shook his head. "I have no idea, Stevie,"

he said. "But people will be talking, and someone must know *something*."

"And what do I do if I manage to get in?" Susan Carol said. "Won't the other players know I'm a fraud right away?"

"Sit in front of an empty locker as if it's yours and listen. There are so many different events going on here at once that no one knows everybody. You never know when you're going to be in the right place at the right time. If we're in three different places, our chances are three times as good of hearing something helpful."

"But what do we think is going on here?" Stevie asked.

"That," Kelleher said, "is the multimillion-dollar question."